Hotel Paradíso

Hotel Paradíso

BY

GREGOR ROBINSON

RAINCOAST BOOKS

Vancouver

Raincoast Books acknowledges the ongoing support of The Canada Council; the British Columbia Ministry of Small Business, Tourism and Culture through the BC Arts Council; and the Government of Canada through the Book Publishing Industry Development Program (BPIDP).

First published in 2000 by

Raincoast Books
9050 Shaughnessy Street
Vancouver, B.C.
V6P 6E5
(604) 323-7100

www.raincoast.com

Edited by Joy Gugeler
Typeset by Bamboo & Silk Design Inc.
Cover design by Les Smith
Cover image by Alex Colville

1 2 3 4 5 6 7 8 9 10

CANADIAN CATALOGUING IN PUBLICATION DATA
Robinson, Gregor.
 Hotel Paradiso

 ISBN 1-55192-358-0
 I. Title.
PS8585.O351625H67 2000   C813'.54   C00-910710-X
PR9199.3.R5345H67 2000

Printed and bound in Canada

For my daughters
Alix and Esmée

Contents

Hotel Inglaterra, Havana, September

Last week I left Pigeon Cay for the last time. Two years — gone. Left the bank, Healey, Tommas. The Hotel Paradiso. Annie. Most of all, Annie.

There was no ceremony to mark my departure. I locked the door to the bank and then the door to my house. Greasy shadows marked the walls where picture frames had hung: drawings of Huron and Dufferin counties (exotic dreamscapes from the vantage of the Tropics); my degree from the London School of Economics; a map of the island and the cays; a picture of the shimmering blue-green sea; a photo of Karen and me on our honeymoon — ironic, of course.

I am no longer the person in the picture. My hair has gone quite grey. Forty-one next month. Not so old. But some of my classmates from graduate school are now heads of faculties, directors of government departments, officials at the World Bank, partners at brokerage and law firms. I imagine their houses are immense. My father was a solicitor, a small-town professional man. I am a banker, but also something else, something less predictable. A writer.

Gregor Robinson

Didn't say goodbye to Annie, couldn't, really. We both knew I was leaving. "All we have is time" — is that what she said? I wonder if fate will be so generous. I long for her to join me in Miami.

I came for escape but found entanglement instead. Is my heart broken, or is this only exhaustion? Relief? Perhaps our affair was corrupt from the start, a way out. Corrupt, like the whole place, the tourists, the drugs, the illegal migrants, the money business. I'd wanted time to write, but needed money to eat, love to live. Sex, anyway — that's how it started with Annie. Perhaps our love grew out of mutual need. A fair exchange. We were quite different, strangers really.

Stopped over in Cuba for a couple of weeks en route to Miami. As if it's more time I need. But the bank's paying; a final, discreet perk. They don't like to be reminded of where the money came from, what we were doing. None of us do. Until I came to the islands, I had never seen a gun. I had never seen a dead body.

I'm staying with Ed Holder, at an apartment he keeps in Old Havana. Last night he said farewell to the latest of his conquests. How many times has this scene been played? The gathering of the woman's things from the bedroom, the solemn repacking. A final U.S.$20 from Ed or Frank or Joe, Emil from Turin, or perhaps one of those loud Russians at the Café Cantante. Any man, to take her away.

And what about those men? What about Ed? Does he think she likes the broken capillaries on his face, the hair on his back, his breath, the flesh at his waist? Does he think that she hasn't heard these words a thousand times before? Did I? Can a person live apart from the world, uncorrupted?

These pages started neither as a journal nor as a confession. They were to be my notes on the flora and fauna of the islands. The amateur naturalist, his dog-eared *Peterson* under his arm; I saw the type occasionally, strolling down the windward side of the island, wearing spectacles, a straw hat.

I shall wear the bottom of my trousers rolled. Shall I part my hair behind? Do I dare eat a peach? I shall wear white flannel trousers, and walk upon the beach.

But I wasn't one of those. Not bloodless, not me, certainly not.

The fascination with plants and animals was the return of a childhood interest that began with pheasants and ladybugs in the spinney behind our house, in the pasture that fell down to the Speed River.

Besides, I was lonely. Late at night in my cottage at the mouth of the harbour with a glass of rum (or two) as I made my notes — it was a diversion and provided a sense of purpose, the scratching of my pen above the noise of the surf to keep me company. A taxonomist's exercise. I was a classifier and a voyeur. But what is that notion in science — the uncertainty principle? How observing a thing changes it forever?

One morning you wake up and you're part of it, part of the story. Sometimes I didn't even see the specimen, the life I was writing about. It was enough simply that there be evidence of its existence, that it *could* exist. Like love.

So, a journal, a story, and now a gift to you.

One

This is a story of a man who came to the islands because he longed for the exotic, to descend like a diver into a different world.

Once I met an Englishman from Kent. For him it was the clear cold north, not the north he knew — Leeds and Bradford — but another kind of north. He yearned for an empty place of ice and tundra, a place to dress in skins and furs. He wanted to go to Baffin Island. Baffin Island? I'd been as far as Smooth Rock Falls, I told him. It had seemed to take all day and once I got there I wanted out, to head south again, to the world I knew.

I wanted another kind of island — palm trees in a southern sea. I believed that people changed by leaving things behind. There would be mild weather and possibilities, languid women on the white sand, dark rum with knobbly limes and oranges. Maybe, in the background (quite far back), someone with a gun, a hint of dark romance. And everywhere you looked the radiant silhouette of palms against a brilliant sky.

But even in my dreams I was not a castaway. A person has to make a living. So the bank paid for the move, gave me a re-location allowance, a simple scam. Karen said it was a joke, said it with a sneer. In her eyes I had grown corrupt.

Gregor Robinson

As the plane from Miami began its descent into the Berry Islands, I gazed out the window at a patchwork airstrip, surrounded by scrub bush. From that altitude, the land looked like the Canadian Shield, like a place I flew into once north of Bancroft. Karen had just joined the band and was doing a tour of dingy bars in northern and eastern Ontario. Sometimes, on a Saturday, I would fly up from Montreal to join her. Karen was always on about her "gigs." I hated that word, used to make fun of it. Sounded like appendages, I said, or one-night stands, which turned out to be closer to the truth. Karen said that I was just a banker. I was mostly doing loans to car dealers then.

We bumped, then taxied to a stop near an abandoned luggage cart. Its sides were shot through with rust, the blue-and-white airline insignia eaten away by the salt air. By the edge of the runway an old DC-3 sat half shrouded in brown canvas, ropes anchoring the wings to the ground. One of the engine cowlings lay in the weeds. A boy with an oily rag in his back pocket gazed into the motor.

The pilot opened the plane door. A blast of hot wind rushed through the cabin — the smell of oil and the sea. I stepped onto the tarmac. I'd been travelling since six that morning, with only a couple of hours at Miami, time enough for three Bloody Marys. The alcohol, the long day, the hot sun: I was drugged.

Near the squat metal terminal a man in white trousers and a pale blue shirt spoke to a black woman. He held a clipboard.

"It's criminal, absolutely criminal," he said. "She should be with her parents."

Next to him stood a woman with a wailing child in her arms.

Our pilot came out of the terminal. He looked harassed. He turned to me and said, "Mr. Rennison?"

I nodded.

"Okay for you to wait here a while? Get another plane, maybe an hour from now?"

You could tell from his tone that he didn't want an argument. He squinted at the sun.

"We've got a kid here who's real sick," he said. "She can sit on her mother's knee but we're still short one seat. You're the last name on the list…." His voice trailed off and he shrugged. He said I could use the radiophone in the terminal to call Healey.

"How will I be getting out?" I asked.

"Plane over there," he said, pointing to the DC-3. I must have looked surprised, because he touched me on the shoulder and added, "She's in great shape."

In five minutes they were gone. I stood alone at the outdoor loading area, drinking a warm soda from the Coke machine, a 1950s model. I sent a message to Healey, then found a bench to catch some sleep.

Perhaps an hour later I was awakened by a jeep skidding to a stop. The driver was lanky, sun-burned, and wore silver-framed, mirrored glasses.

"I'm your pilot. Bob Wade."

He took a duffel bag from the back of the jeep and we walked to the DC-3.

I sat in a jerry-built seat behind Wade, the wall of the cargo compartment close. The boy with the rag in his pocket jammed my luggage behind me, then climbed into the co-pilot's seat.

"Don't usually carry passengers," Wade said. "This is the best we can do."

"What *do* you carry?" I asked.

Wade didn't answer. He said, "We put down at Marsh Harbour. Then you take a boat."

As he spoke, I looked down. A gun slid from underneath

Wade's seat so that it lay between my feet, dull black, almost camouflaged against the plane's metal floor. A long, thin barrel. It was all I could have asked for. I inquired about the weather.

"West wind blowing, rain tonight, maybe tomorrow. After that you should get sunshine."

I told him I was with the bank. We were setting up an out-island branch. We had to appear as though we were serving the people here, I said, not just taking their money and sending it to Montreal.

Originally, they'd planned to run the office from one of the other islands. The branch was only going to be open three days a week, maybe another day and a half in tourist season. But I'd approached the bank and sold them on the advantages of having someone permanently posted, someone who had worked at head office in Montreal and could help with Caribbean and Latin American country analysis. I knew a little Spanish. Merton had been surprised by the request. He was my hot shot boss, younger than I was and already on the 22nd floor. Another reason I wanted to go.

"It's a job more suited to an older guy, someone on the way down," he said. "What are you, burnt out? In your 30s?"

Karen and I were supposed to be living together in Montreal, but she was still with the band, working out of Toronto, when I asked for the transfer. There had been long-distance phone calls. They were always on the verge of some huge recording contract. I hadn't seen her for weeks.

"What about that lady of yours?" Merton had leered. He'd seen Karen at an office party: loose hair, cornflower eyes, open-toed shoes. She had made an impression.

"She thinks it's a great idea," I had said.

But Karen stayed in Toronto. It was a choice she'd made long before I decided to come to the islands.

We began our descent. From the window, I saw Healey standing by the chicken-wire gate at the edge of the runway. He'd come in from Nassau earlier in the week and was staying with the local agent at Marsh Harbour. Healey was responsible for all four of the out-island branches.

The plane shuddered to a stop.

"You need any help?" Wade shouted over the roar of the engines. I shook my head. I had only a single bag.

"No, I mean at the bank," he yelled. "You going to need any help at the bank?"

"It's possible," I said, surprised. "Maybe a teller. I don't know."

He waved. "Yeah, well, you take care now." He pulled the stairs up into the cabin and slammed the door.

Healey wore baggy white slacks that flapped in the wind, white shoes, a vivid blue-and-green flowered shirt and blue aviator glasses. I told him he didn't look like a banker.

"So? It's nearly six. The bank's closed. Welcome to the islands."

Healey was at the bank because his father said he needed experience before joining the family business. They had pulled strings to get him the Caribbean.

"So what took you? I've got a taxi waiting. See the fat guy with the beer, whizzing under the fender? That's our driver. Hey, you're going to love the islands."

The vegetation along the road was low and dry. Not green, not tropical, not lurid. We drove by nodes of bleak, cinder-block developments — a liquor store, a hardware store, a dentist's office — separated from one another by stretches of russet field and scruffy trees.

"How are things here?" I asked Healey. "Ready for business?"

"Ready for business? Christ, what's that supposed to mean? I thought you came down here to get away from that bullshit."

I shrugged.

"Yeah, everything's set. The walls are painted. We got a counter from Barclay's when they closed. The place is small. One room. You want to embezzle, drink on the job, you've got to go out back. You got a great thing going here: no boss, no work. Not much nightlife. Still, better here than Montreal. All you've got to do is land some customers."

Healey wasn't surprised when I came south. He knew what had been going on. Karen had met the guy from California by then, the sort of man I wouldn't understand, she said — a poet.

"A poet?" Healey had laughed. "From California? That's classic. Does he have a ponytail?"

When I met Karen she was training to be a music teacher, primary school — music therapy, actually. Not long after that we moved in together, an old farmhouse north of Toronto, near Newmarket, in the urban shadow where everything is in flux. If you looked south you saw apartment buildings along Highway 11. To the north were fields of corn. Karen laid out an herb garden and tried making fancy fruit jams.

The trouble started when she got into a performance course at night school. She started talking about how she wanted to do more with her life, about how she wanted a change. I didn't understand that then, why someone would want to change.

The taxi took us through town to the ferry dock. The air had suddenly turned cool. Across the channel I could see the steady wink of the Pigeon Cay lighthouse, a rhythmic ten and two. Summer in the West Indies, but the sea was milky green, like Lake Huron in the fall.

Half an hour and a sudden rainsquall later, we glided into Pigeon Cay harbour by the glow of the running lights. The tide was out; we had to watch for sandbars. I could see nothing but the ghostly shapes of sailboats, a dark forest on the far hill and, like a stage set, the jagged outlines of the palm trees.

We climbed the ladder by the hazy light at the end of the pier, then onto a broad and curving paved path, pale in the darkness, with small houses close on either side. The air was warm and heavy with the scent of flowers.

"This is the main street," Healey said. He tapped his foot on the pavement. "The Queen's bloody Highway."

He'd rented a house at the far end of the village where I was to stay until I could make more permanent arrangements. There were no streetlights and the house was dark. We stumbled past the flimsy picket gate and up the path. Inside, there were two beige-and-orange bedrooms and a living room with a kitchen and a counter in one corner. It was like a suite at the airport Ramada.

On the kitchen counter sat a large bottle of rum and a mesh cotton bag of pink grapefruits. A neatly printed note read: "Welcome Dear Mr. Rennison. And to the Bank."

Healey had no idea where it came from. We drank some of the rum and then I showered and went to bed.

Gregor Robinson

The bank was a one-storey white clapboard building, unkempt bougainvillaea and bright oleander on either side of the door. The shutters were open; the windows were without glass. The temperature was 79 degrees and would rise as the day wore on. It was almost September, but how could you tell?

Healey said you could tell because none of the tourists had arrived yet. He said it was too bad we had to work, because the high-proof rum cost only $2 a bottle and there was great dope, whatever you wanted, down at the Riverside Tavern. He knew the markets like the back of his hand. Healey had an MBA from the Wharton School of Finance.

When I walked into the bank that first morning, Healey was at my desk going through papers from his briefcase, a show of activity.

"Someone here to see you," he said. He nodded in the direction of the bench by the front door.

She was a dark woman, mid-to-late 30s, in a flowered yellow dress that clung to her breasts. There was something alluring about her, a muskiness.

"Mr. Rennison," she said, "did you get my present?"

Healey stood up. "I'll be over at the hotel having a coffee." He left by the rear door.

"Yes, I got it last night," I said. "Thank you. Thanks very much."

"Mr. Wade, the pilot, he's a friend of mine. He told me you were coming." She paused, then asked, "Mr. Rennison, do you like children?"

"Children?" I was rather taken aback. "I suppose I do."

"Our children are our future, Mr. Rennison. But it's not so good for children here, not much to do when they grow up. Hard to make sure they get an education. Though I'm sure you know all about that, an educated man like you."

The ceiling fan turned slowly, faintly stirring her glossy hair. She had the brightest teeth.

"Mr. Rennison, I want to make a deposit."

She handed me a crumpled envelope. I counted out $1,500 in American and local bills, mostly 10s and 20s. I noticed that the money smelled.

"Mr. Wade told me that the bank was opening today, so I came right over. You want business, right? I have a lot of friends."

I didn't know who her friends were, but I took the money and passed her along to Winnie to open the account.

The hotel next door was called the Majestic. Healey was sitting by the pool — the Terrace Bar — with a couple of Beck's on the table. "One for you," he said.

Healey said the woman's name was Annie Clare. She ran a little bar, the Goombay, at the other end of the island, toward Tilloo Cay. Not many customers, local fishermen, some of the Haitians who lived in the bush, maybe once in a while big spenders in flashy speedboats from across the channel. The bar wasn't licensed for it, but the owners allowed gambling.

I told him about the money.

"Your first customer. Congratulations," he said. "She wouldn't talk to me. How did she know your name?"

"Wade, the pilot. He called her yesterday afternoon."

"Wade runs drugs. That's probably where the money came from. He needs to use different people to front the cash, do deliveries."

"Money is money."

"Oh, absolutely," said Healey. "Absolutely. But not everyone is as broadminded as we are. You don't want to go mentioning this to anyone else in the bank. Or to Montreal."

"She wants me to give her daughter a job," I said. "Fifteen years old. The girl is coming to see me this afternoon."

"We already have Winnie to work behind the counter. A girl from one of the old white families in the village. It was set up by Nassau — with Burnett's help, of course — you'll meet him later at the Club. Jobs are scarce here. They want to do everything...properly. Of course, it's up to you."

The island school, a pink-shuttered, gingerbread cottage, was set in a grove of wispy casuarinas at the end of the village, perhaps 200 yards from the bank. At noon I heard the chiming of the old-fashioned bell.

"Mr. Rennison?" She stood in my doorway, must have run all the way. She wore the school uniform: a blue tunic and white blouse. Her dark hair was in long braids. Tall, slender, pretty. She was mulatto, much lighter than her mother. She looked at her shoes.

"You must be Annie's daughter."

"Yes, please. I would very much like a job here at the bank, Mr. Rennison, sir." She had a small, hesitant voice.

"What's your name?" I asked.

"Azalea."

"Azalea Clare. A pretty name. Why do you want the job? Are you interested in banking?"

"No, sir. I want to save money for business college, in Nassau. I'm too old to be going to the school here."

"Well, I'm sorry, Azalea. The job is taken."

She shrugged her shoulders, took a few steps across the room and placed a piece of paper on my desk before she left. It was a note of recommendation from her teacher, along with her marks. Straight As.

Another thing: I was expecting the Yacht Club to be wide verandas and faithful servants, stewards in white jackets bringing round the gin on silver trays while the gentlemen played cards and smoked fat cigars. Somerset Maugham country. Instead, you brought your own bottle in a paper bag. The convening committee provided mix, ice cubes, plastic tumblers and a sullen black man at a folding table to set them up. That was on Saturday nights; most other days the place was locked and shuttered. The Club was nothing more than a wooden hut with a covered stone patio at the side. An overgrown trellis protected members from the gaze of curious passersby. The bar in the main room had once been a storage cupboard. Across the road, in a hut identical but for the faded paint and whiff of urine, lived a large family of ragged Haitians, refugees who one night not long ago had stumbled from the sea.

"Pace yourself," Healey advised, as we strolled along the Queen's Highway. Tonight I would meet Burnett, a failed citrus grower and a member of the bank's board of directors. Healey had been briefing me on some of the guests. "Don't get drunk until the rest of them do. When the food comes round, go for it because it's gone in a second. Pigs at the trough."

This was one of the summer racing days, so all the flags were flying: the Stars and Stripes, the red Maple Leaf, the Union Jack.

"Don't look now," Healey whispered as we approached the entrance. "I think we're being followed. Riffraff. Hold on to that bottle."

We passed through the open gate of the trellis and made our way through the crowd. People were dressed in colourful shorts, oxford-cloth shirts, boat shoes. There were only about 30 but the noise level was rising quickly.

"Where is the bar?"

"First things first," said Healey. "I must introduce you to our fearless leader."

Burnett kept the title of vice-chairman, even though he spent most of his time in the islands. Occasionally he flew to Montreal and New York for meetings. He was standing in the centre of the room talking with three others, all in their late 50s. He was tall, with a ruddy face — probably as much from the rum as from the sun — and slicked-back iron-grey hair. He shook my hand, then introduced me to the others.

"Our new man in the village," he said.

"Welcome to Pigeon Cay, Mr. Rennison," said Mrs. Holborne. She was from Connecticut and had a curiously British accent (the way old money talks, Healey said later). "I can't *tell* you how happy we are to have a new face at our little club. Especially someone so young. And handsome." She examined me with a vulture's eye. Mrs. Holborne's third marriage had recently ended because of some trouble with a stable manager. She was one of the seasonal residents and did not usually come to the islands until later; on this occasion she was returning home from Lyford Cay and had stopped in for only the day.

Tom Hargreaves was a balding, ex-Foreign Service officer, with a flaky sun-burned forehead, which he scratched habitually. He had a reputation as a sailor. His wife, Mary, stood beside him, a foot or so behind. Her movements were quick and birdlike. Her hand, when we were introduced, was damp.

"These are your future customers, my boy, if you play your cards right," said Burnett.

"Astonish me," said Mrs. Holborne, "and I am yours."

"Don't see why I should switch over from Marsh Harbour," said Tom Hargreaves, scratching his scaly pate.

"Because it will be so much more convenient," said Burnett.

"You made the arrangements to hire Winnie, the girl behind the counter," I said to Burnett.

"I hope you approve. Winnie is a Macdonald. Old family, one of the ones who settled Pigeon Cay at the time of the American Revolution. She'll bring you business. The Macdonalds must be related to half the people in the village. Her father is the last dinghy builder on the island."

"These local people are so *simple*," said Mrs. Holborne, with a wave of her hand. "So charming."

"What would happen if we hired someone else?" I asked.

"Nothing much. Might annoy some of your potential customers, I suppose." Burnett took a sip of his drink and looked at me for several seconds. "It's up to you, of course. But the paperwork and so forth, that's already been done. Bit of a bother to change horses now."

"Besides," said Tom Hargreaves, "Winnie is white."

"How about that drink?" said Healey, bustling.

"I'm with you there," said Tom Hargreaves. He turned to lead us through the crowd to the bar. "Steady as she goes."

We gave our orders. The barman paused mid-drink and looked over our shoulders toward the door.

"What is it?" I asked.

On the sidewalk outside there was shuffling, a scuffle, angry shouting. The vine leaves on the trellis shook. Someone lunged against the gate.

"It's your first customer," Healey said to me.

It was indeed Annie, accompanied by several young men.

"Let's lie low," I said.

More angry shouting.

"Don't let her through," someone yelled.

A small crowd had started to gather outside the Yacht Club. Some of the Haitians, some of the villagers, even some of the men from the Riverside Tavern were beginning to drift along the walk toward the Club.

"Are we to be caught in some kind of riot?" said Mrs. Holborne. "Too exciting. I simply *cannot* believe it!"

"Tom, should we leave?" Mary Hargreaves said, wringing her hands.

"Steady as she goes," said Hargreaves, edging toward the rear of the terrace.

A group of men gathered around the door. Through the latticework we watched the struggle. Burnett and some of the others were trying to calm Annie. Something flashed in her hand, then the glitter of a bottle traced an arc through the air. The bottle smashed against the doorframe behind me, showering glass at my feet. Dark rum dribbled down my shirt.

"Pigs!" She glared through the fence. The crowd beyond the trellis began to sway and murmur. We faced each other through the vine leaves. At last a couple of policemen arrived. One of them tipped his hat to Burnett.

"All right Annie, come along with me. The rest of you make your way back to the bar. There's nothing to see. Off you go."

Annie's voice faded as she was led into the darkness. The sullen crowd dissipated.

"Rennison," said Burnett, returning from the fray. "Do you know that that dreadful woman out there was asking for you?"

"Really?"

"Any idea what she wanted?"

"None at all, I'm afraid."

What would happen to Azalea now?

"Nothing," Healey said.

I woke late, with a headache. I walked across the narrow hump of land to the Atlantic side of the island. In the sky to the south I watched the silver speck of an airplane shimmering in the sunlight until the drone of the engines faded into the rush of the surf. Above me the fronds of the high palms *click-click*ed in the wind. Something was different, but it wasn't me. It was only these summer days. How different they were from Ontario: the slamming of the wooden screen door, pale dust in the tall grass, the electric buzz of the cicada fading into the afternoon.

Pigeon Cay, June

Out the open window, through the slats of the jalousie and a grove of stubby saw palmettos, I see a pair of rare Bahamian parrots soar across the mouth of the harbour to the hurricane hole where the yachts and fishing boats take cover in the fall. It's really just an open lagoon amidst the mangroves. I rowed there yesterday in the Zodiac, the sound of rank water slurping and sucking in the undergrowth. The swamp traps visitors in their boats. There is no solid ground here.

How different this foliage is from the flickering beech stands, the forests of jack and red pine planted by the Ministry of Natural Resources, the corn and hay fields rolling away from Ontario county roads. Experience must be made of place.

High on the beach near where the sea grapes begin, I saw my first scuttling crabs, the tiny three-coloured hermit, blue legs with white bands and orange joints and the larger, more common land hermit. It occupies the shells of others, a kind of brother.

I have assembled a small shelf of books on the flora and fauna of the islands, plan to do some research, which I may work into the stories.

Gregor Robinson

And this strange, sad business with *Ricinus communis*, family, *Euphorbiaceae*, native to Africa, now at home throughout the Tropics. Spotted it also in Mrs. Holborne's garden, of all places, where it could be watered and carefully tended. Cultivated mainly for its oil — castor oil — although some people do grow the plant solely for its beauty. Surprising, given the risks, although Mrs. Holborne's place is looked after by a team of Haitian gardeners.

The fruit is deep red in colour, bristly, spined, to protect the seeds. It grows in thick clusters, rather like Mrs. Reider's hair in fact. She came into the bank the other day, so cool and remote, seems to cultivate a chill about her, the aura of the expatriate. (Am I, too, becoming melancholy, growing a little strange?) Professional, white, travelled, accomplished, wealthy, tasteful. But she leaves her little girl with the housekeeper while she flies off to meet her lover.

She walked beside me, arm against arm, hip against hip, brushing my skin with her bare arms that day at the beach. Perhaps she was lonely.

The line from Shakespeare: "Men have died from time to time and worms have eaten them, but not for love." A comfort, to be sure, though not always true.

What happened to Mrs. Reider and her daughter is the stuff of fiction. Or is it just because I am distant from their lives, know few of the details, that I can make stories of them? I know nothing of the complexity, the texture of what must have gone before.

All the same, I've seen Mrs. Reider's type. Unlike Annie. She is so different from Mrs. R., her relationship to her daughter. She asked about a job at the bank for Azalea, wanted a means for her to earn her way off the island, a better life. What happens to children like Azalea, when they are cut adrift? To any child?

Perhaps if Karen and I had had a child....We never found any peace and I never grew accustomed to her detachment, our arguments ending in icy silence. I am too close to those events to make of them a story.

This morning I hear the Atlantic crashing on the windward side of the island, though I look out on the quiet, luminescent, blue-green sea.

I am adrift.

Two

"To me, Pigeon Cay is a private hell," said Mrs. Reider. Through the window behind her I could see the green water of the harbour shimmering in the morning sun. The sky was brilliant and cloudless. The windows were open and the wind carried a trace of the perfume of exotic blossoms into the room. At night the windows were battened with wooden shutters to keep out the cold and the hurricanes. If we were to stroll out the door and up the low hill on the other side of the walk — the main street was a paved path; there were no cars in the village — we would come upon the ocean waves crashing on the reef, foaming in long fingers on the white sand.

"I tell you, I'm glad to be leaving." Mrs. Reider sounded exhausted. I noticed for the first time the trace of an accent in her voice. ("She's a Jew," Mrs. Holborne had told me triumphantly, "*of course* she is!")

Mrs. Reider looked away from me and out the window. She was small and olive-skinned, with delicate features. Her hair, deep auburn, was pulled back from her head. She was the most exotic of our group, said by the ladies of the Yacht Club to be able to speak several languages, mostly eastern European, unfortunately. French would have been preferable. She was in her early 40s, only a few years older than me. We were both much younger than the retired lawyers, businessmen, Foreign Service officers and various preserved ladies who made up the expatriate community at Pigeon Cay. They had tans or mottled sunburns, wore clothing in primary colours or pastels, were rich and well groomed. But they were dowdy next to Mrs. Reider, strutting pigeons to her peacock, inappropriate beneath the palm trees.

Most fantastic of all was that the Reiders had actually been prepared to *live* here — not just in the winter, or for the months when the tax laws made it necessary for people to "establish domicile," but all the time. They had bought the Senator's house, next to the cholera cemetery. Exposed to the ocean, but closer to the village than any of us would have tolerated, the Senator's house had always been among the most popular of the tourist rentals. There were spectacular views of the Atlantic from both sides of the point.

The Reiders installed an immense cistern, the first new one to have been built in Pigeon Cay in many years, so that they could have the luxury of a full-sized bathtub and a washing machine. A bright-orange backhoe arrived one morning on a barge from across the channel. The Reiders were not going to send their laundry out to be done by the Haitian women, as the rest of us did. They would make a permanent home here, along with the poor Bahamians, the Haitian refugees, the deranged exiles from Latin America. They would make themselves a life.

In other ways, though, Mrs. Reider fitted the profile: an exile from a bittersweet past, melancholy, cherishing a certain loneliness.

"I didn't know they were poison," Mrs. Reider said. She was still looking away from me, out the window. "I suppose you and the others will never believe that now."

"For what it's worth, I do believe you," I said.

I was lying. It may have been an accident, but I believed she had wanted out, one way or the other; she almost said as much to me that day on the beach. Certainly she had discussed it with the man from Trinidad.

I also agreed with Father McEndrick: all actions are motivated, consciously or not, and all actions have consequences. So she was leaving us for good now, immigrating to Israel, and there seemed little point in belabouring such philosophical distinctions. It would be the last time I saw her.

She had asked me to transfer the balance of her account to a bank in New York and to gather up the necessary documents.

That was something I should have noticed from the beginning — the trouble she and Reider had over money. It's often a sign. They had been in Pigeon Cay about three months when she first visied the bank. She wanted more money. Impossible, I told her, I could not authorize transfers from her husband's accounts to either the joint account or her own. According to the regulations, I should not have revealed to her even that much — that her husband *had* a personal account. But I was lonely. I had spoken with her several times in the village.

She paused, then said, "My husband is away for days, even weeks at a time."

Mrs. Reider said things, told me things about herself that I would have liked to interpret as a kind of invitation. It was not the brassy flirtatiousness you saw among the women at the Yacht Club, the wives of amateur sailors who had made their money and retired early.

Mrs. Reider said, "I sometimes need more than he gives me."

"I'm sorry I cannot help you." I tried to curb a tendency to officiousness in my manner. I came out from behind my desk. "You understand my position, Mrs. Reider. The bank has rules."

I offered to show her what I knew of the island. There was an outboard I could borrow. We would walk through the bush to where the boat was docked; we would taxi to a secluded beach beyond White Narrows.

Several nights later at the Club, I learned that, like her husband, Mrs. Reider had taken to leaving the island alone. It was a Thursday, Ladies' Bridge Night, and the Snug Bar was open. We were at close quarters.

"The last time, she took a water taxi across the channel, not the regular ferry. Two o'clock in the afternoon." This from Mary Hargreaves. Silence made her nervous, so she quickly added, "Tom was down at the harbour fussing with his boat and saw her heading out."

"That would mean she was taking the three o'clock plane," said Grace Wood, whose husband had made a fortune manufacturing plastic mesh baseball caps. She tapped her nose with the pencil; she was the scorekeeper. "That is the plane to Nassau. She must be going some place in the Caribbean. Otherwise she'd have taken one of the later flights, to Florida."

"Probably visiting her husband," said Mrs. Holborne's niece, Hermione, clearly bored. She was visiting from Massachusetts and did not know Mrs. Reider.

"Mr. Reider is in Honduras this week," said Mary Hargreaves, playing her trump. The others eyed her, waiting for more. "Burnett told Tom," she said.

Play continued.

"So? She's having an affair," said Hermione. "So what?"

There was silence at the table. As an outsider, Hermione could not have been expected to know any better.

"I am the last one to cast aspersions," said Mrs. Holborne. "My own youth was not exactly colourless. But there was never a child involved."

"Of course not," said Mary Hargreaves.

"By the time I was Mrs. Reider's age, my children were grown up and away at school," said Mrs. Holborne.

"She is only the stepmother," said Grace Wood.

"All the same," said Mrs. Holborne.

"So where do you suppose she goes on these little jaunts?" Grace Wood asked.

The bartender handed me my drink. The three older women looked over at me. I sipped my rum and grapefruit and gazed at the ceiling fan.

Boat rides and picnics at quiet beaches were among the few diversions we could offer visitors to Pigeon Cay. There was only the single road on the island and nowhere much to go on that. On other islands there were condominiums and casinos, ponies and wild pigs, giant iguanas and snakes, dense forests to get lost in. But not here. Not on Pigeon Cay. The only true wildlife I'd seen was a black rat on the government pier.

I made my way through a pack of stray dogs and up the path to the Senator's house. The child answered the door. In her hair was a red hibiscus blossom.

"I'm six," she said. "I have a sore." She held out her hand so that I could inspect the bandage, grey and fingered.

"Shall I kiss it better?" I asked.

"Will I have to take the bandage off?"

"Certainly not," I answered.

She held out her hand again. She had brown eyes like her father's. Otherwise she was small and dark, like her mother. After I kissed her hand, she inspected me. She chewed on a long gold necklace, which she wore around her neck.

A black woman appeared from the kitchen and whisked the girl away. I waited in the whitewashed living room. It was sparsely furnished and smelled of disinfectant. Mrs. Reider came down the narrow stairs. Her hair was held back in a knotted silk scarf. She wore crisp cotton slacks, a cream-coloured blouse and a string of irregular beads, mottled black and brown and white. I thought she looked elegant, but overdressed for a boat ride and a picnic.

By the door she picked up a net bag, which held her bathing suit, a towel, a pack of Marlboro cigarettes. I didn't move until she said, "The child will not be coming with us." That was how she referred to her, "the child." She said that the sea would be too cold.

"The sea is not at all cold," I said.

But Chloe had been ill, she said, and Mr. Reider had left strict instructions that she not be allowed into the water.

We walked along the dusty road from the village, then turned off on a trail that took us past the Haitian refugee settlement, along the back of the harbour, through the swamp, Fish Mangrove. Tiny succulent oysters at one time grew on the roots and skeins of the mangrove here, but poisons from the engines and toilets of the gleaming yachts in the harbour had made them extinct. Now rank algae bloomed in the lagoon and pulsating jellyfish flourished. We trod over soggy bits of paper, plastic bottles, used condoms.

Past the swamp we entered the woods and walked for an

hour before emerging from the shadows into the garden of the house called Pigeon Point, home of the outboard.

We puttered up the low coastline, bobbing in the slight swell of the afternoon sea. I pointed out the house of the famous actor from New York, the tower in the forest that had been put up by a land developer from Nassau, the places where freighters had foundered, the rocks and coral outcrops. The wind was swinging around from the east and the rage between the outer islands was strong, making it possible for us to venture beyond the lee of Pigeon Cay.

Just beyond the narrows — we heard the Atlantic crashing on the other side — I beached the boat in the sand. The sky had grown overcast, the water grey. We didn't swim. After spreading the picnic blanket and setting out the lunch, we sat side by side on the beach, facing the sea.

Mrs. Reider was silent.

"You've been away," I said. She looked at me as if to ask a question. "In Pigeon Cay, news travels fast."

"I was in Trinidad," she said.

This was June. It was too late for Carnival, but she had been once before. "Did you wear a costume?" I asked. "Join the parades, the dancing in the streets?"

"Only for one night." She touched the sombre beads around her neck in a way that reminded me of the little girl. "The southern islands. Much more life."

"It's the Latins," I said, "people from South India, especially Africans. This island, on the other hand, was settled by the same Puritans who settled New England."

Her eyes were red-rimmed. I put my hand on her arm, but she turned and gave me a stony look.

"Allergies," she said. "My husband travels a great deal," as though it were that to which she was allergic.

Her husband was a consultant, an engineer who specialized in hydraulics and the handling of liquids — oil, chemicals, even the black molasses shipped north and turned into rum.

She said, "I know what they're saying at the Club. That I met a man there, in Trinidad. It's true."

At the Yacht Club, opinion began to shift. The husband was away too much. She was lonely. She needed companionship. Reider had been seen at the airport in Freeport with another woman.

"When mine behaved like that, my second one, Mr. Norman — the children always called him Mr. Norman although in point of fact his name was Schlumburger — I confronted him at once," said Mrs. Holborne. "I did not moon about. I did not travel. I did not take a lover. I simply told him to go. I believe I may have thrown something. A piece of glass, a little sculptured thing."

"He was your second. It might have been different had you married later in life," said Grace Wood.

"I did marry later in life," said Mrs. Holborne.

"I meant for the first time," said Grace Wood.

Mary Hargreaves said, "The husband travels on business. He can't be blamed for that." As a rule, Mary Hargreaves believed worse of wives than of husbands.

Mrs. Holborne paused, a Campari and soda halfway to her lips. "Of course, my dear." She returned the glass to the table. "Opportunity. In my experience, that is what business trips are to men."

It was Sunday, a regatta luncheon behind the flowered trellis. We were waiting for the boats to come in. The Reiders were not present. To the committee's immense surprise, Reider had declined an invitation to let their names stand for membership. This had never happened before. One couple had been black balled — real estate agents from Toronto — but no one had ever declined.

At first the problem was taken for a severe cold or flu. Father McEndrick, a Bahamian, came into the bank the day she fell ill. "Perhaps you have noticed her," he said. The children often came down the road at recess, at lunchtime, or at the end of the school day. They paraded by my open door, most of them locals who lived in the north end of the village where the houses were small and old and in need of a coat of paint.

"A dark-haired little girl. She wears a flower in her hair," said Father McEndrick. "They think it's Mrs. Johnson's fault." The nanny. She had allowed her to go swimming. Father McEndrick knew Mrs. Johnson from the parish.

"You might go over to the house, see what you can do. The family is one of yours." Father McEndrick was black and I was white, but what he meant was that the child was from an expat family.

For the second time I made my way through the stray dogs to the house on the point. The wind had continued strong for days; it howled around the house and though the palms.

Reider answered the door. He said nothing. Mrs. Reider stood by the living room window, looking out to the ocean. Mrs. Johnson sat on an old cane chair in the breezeway to the kitchen. She was holding her stomach, swaying back and forth. She moaned, as though she were the one who were ill. She had been weeping.

"Ignorant woman," Reider muttered.

"How did it start?" I asked.

"Said she had a sore mouth. A burning in the mouth. An hour or two later, diarrhoea. You're no doctor. Can't we get the bloody doctor?"

The doctor arrived as darkness was falling. She had flown in from Eluthera and raised the ferryman at Marsh Harbour. She crossed the dark water to comfort us.

"Poison," she said, after a quick examination. She could not say how serious. The child would have to be moved to better medical facilities, by air from Great Abaco probably. By this time Father McEndrick had arrived. He and Reider brought the girl downstairs. She was shrunken and white. Her eyes fluttered and her head occasionally rolled from side to side. The hibiscus blossom in her hair was bloodred. Around her neck she wore the ugly, tick-shaped beads, mottled black and brown and white.

I leaned toward her. The beads were light, which surprised me. They were slippery to touch, as though coated in wax. I remembered her coming to the door, asking me to kiss her hand, watching me, the gold necklace in her mouth.

"She's been chewing the beads," I said.

Mrs. Reider turned quite pale. I thought for a moment she might faint. "The beads," she whispered.

The Crown wanted the matter treated as criminal, but Burnett, Hargreaves, Mrs. Holborne, didn't want this kind of thing in Pigeon Cay. Besides, the tide had shifted; there was sympathy for Mrs. Reider now.

Mrs. Reider turned from the window. She began to gather up her bags. She put her papers into her purse.

"Where did the poison come from?" I asked. In my journal, I had noted: *The toxin is ricin, from the seed of the castor-oil plant. The ingestion of two to six of the small seeds may be fatal.*

She did not answer.

I asked: "Where did the beads come from?"

"They were a present," she said. "From my friend. He gave me the beads at Carnival. We were drinking, joking. 'You just scrape them like this,' he said," — she motioned with her hand.

The bell of the village school rang, not the piercing ring of an electric bell, but the *ding-ding* of a country school, then children's voices, a ball bouncing on the sidewalk.

Mrs. Reider had been described by the magistrate in New Providence as "negligent." It was the nanny, Mrs. Johnson, who had actually given the beads to the child. She would let the girl wear her mother's clothes and jewellery on those long afternoons when the Reiders had flown off to meet their lovers. She would plait the child's hair, entwining there a blossom from the red hibiscus.

Mrs. Reider stood to go. She clutched her purse in front of her. She looked like a little girl herself. She handed me the slip of a paper with her forwarding addresses. She shook my hand.

"Thank you for your help."

I said nothing. My help had been only that of a functionary.

Gregor Robinson

Mrs. Reider left by the back door in order to avoid seeing the children from the school. I watched her make her way down the path beneath the frangipani to the government pier. I heard the rumble of the engines. The noon ferry waited for her there in the bright lagoon.

Pigeon Cay, August

The weather continues steamy. Hargreaves has agreed to lend Healey and me his rental house on the coast. It is built high on the ridge and gets the sea breezes. A blessing in this heat.

Around the shore of the lee side of the island, the sea side, grows the poisonwood tree, *Metopium toxiferum*. Its smooth firm leaves, dark on the underside and shiny on top, camouflage the danger beneath an innocent canopy of green. You must wear gloves when handling the branches and leaves because even the touch of the white sap raises long dark welts. This I learned too late. At the village clinic, they gave me calamine lotion, but it did no good.

There are more than a hundred species of trees to the square mile, but they are low and light, even inland. The virgin forest was thick and over 60 feet high. When Columbus landed at San Salvador, he wrote, "The trees are as green and leafy as those of Castille in the months of April and May." Not any more.

What was it like in these subtropical islands a thousand years ago, before the Spaniards came from Hispanola, with their dogs and their appetites? The record of change and invasion is more indelible here than on the continents. Coasts and edges show the effects of migration, the ceaseless flow of refugees at the fringes of the Third World and the First. Men and women, young, black or mulatto, poor and without proper papers, as in Thailand, Indonesia, Cuba, the Philippines.

Against my better judgement, I agreed to meet Winnie, our teller, and Vero, the bartender from the Majestic Hotel, at the Riverside Tavern for a drink. When I arrived Annie was there.

She must have arranged it with Winnie. She wore white Capri pants, open-toed sandals, a sleeveless yellow blouse. Hair upswept. She spoke to the Cuban waiter in fluent Spanish; she also speaks French. She occasionally brushed my thigh with her hand. (Did I imagine it?) She left early, to pick up Azalea from her grandmother's house, where she goes after school.

A day to two later Burnett mentions that I've been seen with a black woman. A warning? Less than subtle. Considering the length of time he's been away from Montreal, it's amazing that anyone pays attention to Burnett. I more or less wrote him off when I first met him, but I should have noticed a certain deference among the members of the Yacht Club. He likes to hold forth, while the sea breezes rustle the trellis and stir the bougainvillaea. The Club is just a watering hole with colonial pretensions. Still, I have a feeling that they rather look down on Healey and me; they are rich and retired, after all, and we still work. But I know about their finances; I know details about their lives that would astound them. Other facts I infer.

For my stories, I'm selecting, creating, arranging details to suit the narrative. So in the story about Bonita — in trying to make sense out of certain events — I fictionalize what happened to Healey. (It could only have happened to Healey!) Showed the story to Tommas, the Haitian fellow who writes poetry. He asked what it was about; I said it was something I was working on, just a story. He said it was about retribution, that all stories reflect a moral perspective. Perhaps I will show him others.

Hippomane mancinella (common name, manchineel), genus *Euphorbiaceae*. I found it in the hot and steamy lagoon. A species I've never seen before; on most of the islands it was sought out and burned generations ago. It survives near the coast only in certain remote areas, tangled swamps, where the branches and the fruit — about an inch across, rounded and yellow-green in colour — fall to the still waters and rot. The sap of the manchineel causes severe contact dermatitis, consisting of weals, blisters and arrhythmia, ultimately and quickly leading to skin necrosis. The toxin of the fruit in the bloodstream can cause death.

Three

Bonita was the name of a local girl and also the name of a tree, which was appropriate.

Bonita daphnoides, genus M*yoporaceae*, also not common, found mostly on Exuma, Cat Island and Inagua and in the Guianas and Cuba.

Except for the swaying palms that haunted my dreams, all the trees of the subtropics looked the same at first; they were pale and insubstantial compared with the dark growth of Ontario. There is no virgin forest left, neither pine nor mixed broadleaf. Then I learned that some trees could cause hot rashes and running sores. Some could make a person pale and sick with chills and fever. Like an onion, the surface kept peeling away. I was becoming compulsive, winkling out the secrets of the living things packed within. I was left not with shimmering and exotic islands, but some place hot, dense and as real as a bad itch.

I started to know the difference, to see in a different way. I'd make notes in the back of my journal while Healey lolled with a tall rum and fruit juice in a frosted glass.

Gregor Robinson

It was late summer in the islands; the breezes would be coming soon. Healey had announced that he had to get out of New Providence, an island 70 miles to the south; his house was insufferably hot. I needed a place to stay, for after months of cajoling the workmen were coming from across the channel to replace the cistern and I would be without water for several weeks. It was too early for the tourists, so Hargreaves had agreed to lend us his property at Pigeon Point for a couple of months. In return, we had agreed to help him open up the house and clean the property. Hurricanes had strewn debris everywhere and the house had stood empty for months.

Pigeon Point. Pigeon Cay. Why pigeon, I asked Hargreaves? Why not Palm Point?

After the pigeon plum, he said. That was the first species I learned. Later, I discovered that there are even many kinds of palm trees. The coconut palm and the tall royal palm, planted for the benefit of the tourists, grew high on the ocean side of the island. Inland and on the lee side, the stubby round top, the saw palmetto (brought by the tides and in the guts of seabirds) and the pond top, the bark and leaves of which fell everywhere. You didn't want the bark rotting on the ground, fouling up the garden.

"What's the difference?" said Healey, with a sweep of his hand. Sunlight filtered through the canopy of leaves like golden dust.

Healey stopped working to take a drink. He had prepared an exotic mixture of high-proof rum, lime juice and sweet coconut syrup. He was forever stopping while Hargreaves and Abel, the hired man, worked ceaselessly. I was on the roof, throwing old shingles into large baskets on the ground below. In a tiny pool of water in the eaves trough by my side, a water bug floated languidly.

All morning we gathered branches and cuttings from the rocky garden and paths in front of the house. We made a ragged pile; from there, Abel and his mule hauled the debris through the woods to a fire that sent oily smoke curling up above the treetops.

Except for the roving dogs, Abel's mule was the only domestic animal on the island. Mrs. Holborne had brought a horse over one year to amuse her grandchildren when they came from Connecticut at Christmas, but she'd shipped it back; the cost of maintenance was too much even for her. Grass will not grow on the islands and the cost of bringing hay was more expensive than flying in fresh prime beef from Palm Beach. Abel's mule survived because, like a goat, it ate the pigeon plums, the rinds of old fruit, the roots of peculiar shrubs.

People said that Abel had a way with nature. He had the mule, several dogs and an orchard of papayas, limes and avocados that thrived where none had before. He knew the islands; his family had been here for 200 years. He was short and strong and he rarely spoke.

After lunch we climbed to the roof to hammer in the new shingles. From there you could look down to the sea bottom. This side of the island was chiselled coral rock, sharp and porous; there was no sand nor rollers nor gurgling streams to cloud the radiant green water.

Healey stood and pointed. "Look," he shouted.

Around the bay, close to shore, there came a shadow, languid and undulating. The shadow circled, swam lazily beneath the slats of the pier, then circled back toward us again.

Healey scrambled across the shingles to the ladder. Suddenly, he was on the deck with Hargreaves' gun. Shots like muffled *pops*. There were two tiny *pings* on the water, then, just below the surface, the thrashing of the giant ray. Wounded, it headed out toward the channel and the open sea. Healey fired again and missed.

"Put that damn thing away. It's not a toy," Hargreaves spoke in a strangled voice and Abel stared at Healey with a look of more than mere contempt. With Abel, it was sometimes hard to tell. His eyes were pink and usually flat. I asked him what would happen to the ray.

"Swim across the channel to the swamps to die," he said, "if the sharks don't get him."

Abel must have built up immunity to the sap of the poisonwood tree: I noticed he didn't wear gloves.

Bonita arrived wearing a long, flowered skirt and a white T-shirt with a picture of the lighthouse across her small breasts. Her hair was straight and black; her eyes dark and almost oriental, part Arawak I liked to imagine, the fabled tribe that was here before Columbus. There must be some of the blood still in the islands, though the people have been gone for hundreds of years, cut down by disease and empire. Bonita was slim and moved like a dancer.

"Jesus," said Healey. He went inside to change into a clean shirt and his white linen pants.

She was perhaps 15 years younger than Healey, maybe 22 or 23 years old.

"You'll be wanting someone to help around the place," Tom Hargreaves had said. "How would it be if I arrange for the girl to come in twice a week? Abel's sister. She says she's interested."

That morning she cleaned the house until it was spotless. At Healey's invitation, she stayed on for lunch. On the terrace she smiled from under downcast eyes. Her perfume was of some exotic plant, orange blossom perhaps.

Healey moved in with what he called his full-court press; he was sure no woman could resist.

"The light in your eyes is like the stars," he said to her as she was preparing to leave. "No matter what happens, Bonita, I must see you again. I simply must."

Total bullshit. I told him so after she left.

"All's fair in love and war," said Healey.

"You come up with that yourself?" I said.

After that she came regularly on Wednesday mornings and Friday afternoons, when I was at the bank. I believe Healey arranged this schedule with some care. He was supposed to be working — taking the MacKee across the channel every morning to the office that ran the branches in the out islands — but whenever I came home he was there.

One morning I was awakened by furtive rustlings, bare feet on the wooden floor, whispers. I saw her through the jalousies of the bedroom door. She was dressing and her back was toward me.

"Why so secretive?" I said to Healey. "Did you think I wouldn't approve?"

He shrugged his shoulders. "She's the one that wanted to keep things quiet, not me."

But he must have told her I knew, for after that she stayed over more often and was around the house when I was home. The house was cleaner than it had ever been; she was constantly busy. Healey would lie in the hammock on the terrace, while she shelled peas into an iron pot, or darned his socks, or pressed our sheets and trousers, my shirts neatly folded in my drawer. The refrigerator was always filled: baked chicken, a loaf of home-made bread, a salad of conch and lime juice.

One day she brought us something we never had in the islands: fresh meat, pink and tender. Duck, from the marshy inlets on the large island at the far end of the archipelago, she said, secret lagoons. Abel shot the birds in season, then kept them dressed and frozen. Neither Abel nor Bonita would say exactly where the locals hunted, though Healey offered cash if she revealed the secret.

At the Terrace Bar the next day Healey said, "Look at *those*. Jesus."

Hermione sat at the far end of the pool, reading a fat paperback novel.

"She's staying with Mrs. Holborne," I said.

"Even better," said Healey.

He was thrilled to be included in Mrs. Holborne's dinner invitation, which Seymour Dufresne brought to the office three days later.

I worked late that evening; we were to go to the dinner straight from the bank. Healey arrived wearing a white suit. He reeked of Old Lime.

We docked at Sandy Inlet and crossed the isthmus by the path through the casuarina trees. Beyond the ridge, the Atlantic rollers crashed on the sand, ashy grey in the dusk. Mrs. Holborne's house was a sprawling place of cedar and glass. To one side was the tennis court, out buildings and a couple of golf carts, which Mrs. Holborne and her guests used to travel to the village. Behind the house was the swimming pool.

"What a spread," said Healey. We made our way toward the gate.

"David, how nice of you to come. And this must be your friend, Mr. Healey, is it?"

For a woman with such a fabled past, Mrs. Holborne had a placid exterior. She never fully opened her eyes.

"Mrs. Holborne, good evening," said Healey. "What a wonderful house. And how awfully nice of you to include me."

I looked at Healey with surprise. I was used to his languor and boredom, not oily charm. Positively slick.

"Mmm," said Mrs. Holborne. She glanced down her nose at him. "But you really should be thanking Hermione. She saw you at the hotel, I think?" Mrs. Holborne preferred to phrase things as questions. "Mr. Healey, may I present my niece."

"Hi." Hermione spoke with a nasal New England honk and she made the word into two syllables. She turned to Healey and said it again. *Haw-igh*. Then she flounced away.

In the rooms behind us, servants bustled, setting out food and drinks. There was lobster, roast beef, rolls and, as in the refrigerator at home, conch salad with hot peppers and lime.

There were six other guests and I saw at once why Healey and I had been invited. Apart from Hermione, we were the only people under 60. There were plenty of young people in the islands, but not of the sort for Mrs. Holborne's niece.

At dinner I sat across from Hermione. She wore a silk dress with a loose halter-top. When she leaned forward, one elbow on the table, her hand near her mouth, I could see her breasts. She had a way of laughing that began with a whoop and ended in giggles, as though she were running out of breath.

After dinner there were two tables of bridge. Hermione and Healey offered to sit out. "You go ahead," Healey said to me, all gallantry. "Hermione and I will walk on the beach."

"Fantastic," said Hermione.

When they returned an hour later, they sat on the terrace facing the ocean, drinking beer from clear bottles.

I accompanied Mrs. Holborne to the front door when the other guests rose to leave. Mrs. Holborne reached across and took my wrist. "Why don't you stay, have a swim in the pool.

There are bottles of beer in the kitchen." She waved her hand, then turned down the hall toward her bedroom.

As I strolled into the living room, I heard laughing: Healey's guffaw, Hermione's honk and giggle. They were standing by the French doors. Healey had an arm around her neck. They stood there clinging to one another, swaying and laughing. Healey turned and gave her a peck on the cheek. Then he slipped his hand beneath her halter-top; the thing slithered off and she was naked to the waist. More hooting and giggling. They turned to the French doors. As they crossed the floodlit terrace the dress fell to her ankles. Healey stumbled along as he lifted one foot, then the other; he wrestled with his pants, threw his shirt into the night. Two moonlit bodies raced for the pool. I heard a splash and turned to walk home.

As I passed by the kitchen door, there came a fragrance, sweet and fading: orange blossoms.

Several mornings later Healey appeared early, dressed for tennis.

"Expecting a busy day at the office?" I asked.

"They need a fourth at the Holborne's." He gulped his orange juice without sitting.

After that he was often away. If it wasn't tennis, it was a fourth at bridge, or windsurfing on the sea side of the island, or taking Hermione and Mrs. Holborne to Sandy Cay in the MacKee to snorkel at the reef. There were cruises on the Hargreaves' sloop and barbecue dinners on the beach. There was deep-sea fishing from a boat belonging to one of the Colombians. Several nights he didn't come home at all.

"That fellow, Healey," said Mrs. Holborne, "such beautiful manners. But such a *scoundrel*. When is he going back to Nassau, or wherever it is he is from?"

It was a Friday morning at the bank; Mrs. Holborne was at last to become a customer. She knew Healey was a friend of mine, but she didn't care if she insulted him.

"I understand he's friendly with some of these...," she waved her hand in the air, "*native* girls."

"When is your niece returning to the States?" I asked.

"Sooner than she thinks," said Mrs. Holborne.

Healey was out when I arrived home. Bonita was finishing the cleaning; I asked her if he had left any message, if she knew where he was. She shrugged her shoulders. A few moments later she came onto the veranda where I was reading *The Miami Herald*, to give notice. I would be sad to see her go.

Later, dozing in the armchair, I was roused by the clatter of pots and pans. When I came to the kitchen door, Healey put up his hands and barred the way.

"No, no. Can't come in. Big surprise. We have any wine left? A nice red? You have a look, will you?"

He bustled me out of the room.

An hour later, seated and with the wine poured, Healey brought in the plates. Panfried potatoes and boiled beans with a few red peppers. The meat was succulent and tender, a little like beef fillet.

"Duck," said Healey, beaming. He'd finally managed to get Abel to take him hunting. They had gone to the lagoon early that morning. Abel had left Healey with the shotgun to wait for the sun. He had stood in the swamp in Abel's leaky waders for a couple of hours. Abel returned to pick him up at around nine o'clock.

"Where is this place?" I asked. Healey swore me to secrecy, then showed me on the chart.

I was awakened by screaming. I leapt from my bed and stumbled along the dark hallway toward a sliver of yellow light that shone beneath the door of Healey's room. He was sitting up in bed, the covers at his feet, staring at his body with horror. His legs were no longer legs; they were black and swollen trunks, elephantine. The skin was burned like charbroiled meat.

I tried to reach Dr. Cutter on the radiophone, but she was at Little Harbour and wouldn't be back until the following day. I managed to get Healey to lie down, with a damp cloth on his forehead. The fever seemed to be rising. For the distended skin of his legs, all I could offer was cream from a tiny tube of cortisone, but when I touched him he cried in pain. Toward morning I tried again; as I dabbed at the skin with cotton, a piece of his flesh came off in my hand. Healey moaned, a wave of nausea swept over me.

When Dr. Cutter arrived at noon he was delirious. "He's too sick to move," she said. "He'll have to stay here." She sent Seymour back to the clinic to pick up medicine and equipment. "It could be poison. How do you feel?"

I told her about the duck dinner, but I felt fine. She stared at Healey's legs; she had never seen anything like it. It was as though he had walked through raging fire or been sprayed with acid.

Dr. Cutter sat by Healey most of the night. I brought food and cold drinks and kept her company. By Sunday, he was well enough to be moved to the village clinic. He began to improve. In the middle of the following week a female friend (whom none of us knew) came to pick him up. She had dark hair, glossy and hennaed, and said she had a small plane across the channel. Healey hobbled across the road to the government pier where a water taxi waited. His legs were no longer black and swollen; the blisters had gone, but the skin was still raw.

I was loading suitcases and books into the MacKee, preparing to move from Pigeon Point, when Abel came by in a tin boat. He helped Bonita onto the pier with her buckets and cleaning fluids, then sped away.

"That was excellent duck," I said. "Any chance of more?"

She stared at me. "No, Mr. Rennison. Not for you." She turned up the path to the house.

Seagulls. That's what I think Healey actually shot. He wouldn't know the difference. He wouldn't know that there were no ducks in the islands in August. Nor would he know about the manchineel tree.

Dr. Cutter said that Healey was lucky to be alive. All his life his legs would ache in steamy weather; the skin would turn rough and scaly like the skin of some cold-blooded creature that lived in the stinking waters of the dark lagoons.

Pigeon Cay, December

I'm writing these notes at the office: the ceiling fan turns, the yellow banana quits flutter and chirp at the window, Winnie assiduously files her nails. Business is growing, but not fast enough to keep me occupied. Just as well. Have even jotted down some notes for the new stories; my agent in Boston has been encouraging. Mentioned to her that I'm interested in someone, she wondered if I might use it. But it's only in these pages that I can write my thoughts about Annie; they are private.

Sharks off the reef today and an offshore breeze. The weather is cool and changeable, which keeps the tourists off the beach. This morning, a man in Bermuda shorts approached as I was having my roll and coffee at the Majestic, asked where he could buy some hash. People on holidays think they can get away with anything. The palm trees cast a curse on visitors; they act badly on the whole. It's the romance of the white sand, the vulgar blossoms, the moon and stars over the Atlantic; it's something in the tropical nights, the African and Latin rhythms from boom boxes and radios, from behind the shutters of bars and restaurants. They can't help themselves.

Gregor Robinson

December and already the days are growing shorter like a northern winter. The warmth makes the darkness exotic. Christmas seems inappropriate, the absence of ice and snow, the garish colours. There's no real spiritual presence, though I've never been much of a believer myself. Faith has always seemed to have as much to do with fear as anything else. Still, I'd like to attend a service on Christmas Eve, don't know where yet. Father McEndrick is a truer soul, but Drover is supposed to be the better preacher and he is pressuring me to attend. Besides, he deals with the bank....

Another party at Mrs. Holborne's last night, endless chatter about the possibility of a new hotel on the southern tip: Frank Lloyd Wright on acid; cedar columns, waterfalls and trailing plants falling from stepped, flat roofs. Inappropriate, said Mrs. Holborne, far too large. In the architect's plans there are what look like guard towers around the perimeter. We're not as bad as Jamaica yet, but there *have* been robberies, rapes, scuba divers gone missing.

Mrs. Holborne prefers places like the small Inn at White Narrows that advertises in *The New Yorker*, quaint, illusory. The Majestic is currently our grandest hotel, if rather dowdy. It sits on a small rise, almost in the centre of the island, with a view of both the ocean, with its white sand beach, and the harbour, with its famous striped lighthouse. The harbour side is obscured from the prying eyes of people on the yachts by a carefully planted barricade of royal palms and casuarinas. The front door is modest and faces directly onto the Queen's Highway.

But across the Highway are the swimming pool and the Terrace Bar. From early to mid-morning, coffee and rolls are served, mostly to the locals. At lunch, the rum drinks begin to flow and the place is filled with hotel guests. At the cocktail hour and into the evenings everyone gathers there, it is the centre of island life and the place where I first saw the worm in the apple. You have to wonder what the motive is with a woman like Daphne. I mean to record the events simply, without implying that they had to turn out in any particular way. But Daphne reminded me of Karen. When she first arrived, I couldn't help looking at her. Will it be possible to tell a story about Daphne without making a judgement?

I walk home from Mrs. Holborne's by the light of a yellow paper moon. The windows cast a yellow glow. I am a visitor in a foreign land.

Four

Her disappearance made her more exotic, like an erotic dream about someone you know. For days afterward you see the person in a different light. Loneliness, like fear, makes a person alive to sensation.

I met Daphne the first morning of her visit, a Thursday. I was making coffee at the counter that faced the living room when she came out of the guest room. She wore the briefest of white panties, with tiny blue satin bows at the sides. Nothing else. Already she had a tan. Her hair was black and thick and she wore it shoulder length. She was partway across the room before she noticed me. With a languid gesture, she brushed aside the hair that fell across one eye.

"Hello," she said. Breathy. Trouble.

She continued across the room. She was lean and tall and made no attempt to cover herself. She had a wide mouth and generous lips.

A few days earlier, Healey had called from Nassau on the radiophone: Would I mind putting up some friends of his for a few nights, a couple? They had arrived in the islands early; it was Christmas and the hotel would be full until their room reservations came due. He'd hired a boat and brought them over the previous evening. They were asleep by the time I came in.

For the first few days I didn't see much of them. Thursday I worked late, Friday I took the ferry across the channel and flew to Miami for the day. At night and in the mornings, I could hear them moving in their room, seldom speaking. When I came in late, I would see Daphne's expensive black-frame sunglasses open on the counter, her Bain de Soleil, her sandals, supple and bleached by the sun, in the middle of the room.

In the bathroom, his shaving kit was hidden above the medicine chest. His name was Larry. He was a real-estate lawyer. They had come to the islands because they were trying to recover from something. Healey thought it might have had to do with a photographer. Daphne modelled, part-time.

After breakfast on Saturday, Daphne and I walked down the road to Drover's store. Drover overcharged and carried a limited selection of goods, but the place was clean and nearby, which was more than you could say for the other grocery stores on the island. Above the boxes of fruit, above the freezer, above the shelves of bottles and tinned goods, were hand-printed lessons on the virtues of the Christian way of life. The sign by the tonic water read: NO MATTER HOW DARK AND LONELY THE ROAD, THE LORD WALKS WITH YOU.

"Oh, Christ," said Daphne, "look at *that*." She laughed easily.

Drover glanced in our direction, his glasses glinting in the light of the fluorescent lamp. He was a lay preacher at the Evangelical Church. On the cash register there was a faded news clipping of the burning of Yorkminster Cathedral and above it, written with a felt pen, the words, "God's will be done."

As we were checking out, Drover said, "You be coming Christmas Eve, Mr. Rennison?" He had a soft, nasal voice.

I said I expected I would. Drover nodded, unsmiling. He avoided looking at Daphne. She was wearing a short pink jersey dress, belted with a white sash at the waist, loose at the front. She wore her sunglasses on a silver cord. I never saw her without those glasses around her neck. I have them still.

Larry, Daphne and I lunched on the terrace, overlooking the entrance to the harbour. Daphne ate voraciously and with gusto, sucked her fingers dry. Larry was more fastidious: he picked away at his chicken and concentrated on the gin. They hardly looked at one another.

"So whose idea was it to come down here?" I asked. An innocuous remark, to get the conversation going, but Daphne glared at Larry.

"Don't look at *me*," she said. "It was *his* idea."

After lunch I offered Daphne a section of the paper.

"I don't read newspapers," she said. "I don't like to get my hands dirty." Larry looked up.

"Daphne never knows what's going on." He had brought a copy of *The Economist*.

"Right. I'll get the dessert," I said, bustling. "Fresh fruit."

In the afternoon I took them to the museum, a little house that had been bought and refurbished with the help of donations from members of the local community, both the expatriates and those whose families had been on the island for generations. The attendant was a black man, too timid to say anything when Daphne, disobeying the signs, picked up fragments of crockery for a better look. She perused the rusting tools and old fishing gear, the strange implements that had once been used to make rope, the pieces of calico and old clothing.

"Junk," she said.

At the craft shop Daphne tried on straw hats, handmade by the woman who sat on a chair by the door, fanning herself, watching. Daphne turned from the mirror toward us, one arm against her hip.

"What do you think?" she asked.

"How much?" said Larry.

"Seventeen dollars." She tossed the hat back on the shelf.

The old woman by the door didn't move, didn't blink. Daphne had been on the island three days, but already the people in the village knew her.

Afterward Larry strolled to the Terrace Bar with his newspaper. Daphne said she was going to the beach on the ocean side of the island. She'd already changed. Over her bathing suit she wore a thin white kimono; the folds moved with the sway of ..er hips.

Late Sunday afternoon Drover came to see me. He was accompanied by the large black woman who was his assistant at the church, several siblings and cousins and two other local people. A deputation. They looked grim.

"Mr. Rennison," he said, "that woman, she been going topless on the beach. We got children around here. You got to talk to her. She's your guest. It ain't right. It ain't Christian."

"Right," I said. "I'll speak to her tomorrow." I went to shut the door. Nobody moved.

"Mr. Rennison, you got to talk to her now."

"All right. I'll talk to her now." As they walked away, I heard Drover muttering about the Lord.

I found Daphne on a lonely stretch of sand, far from the hotel; she had not sought out a conspicuous spot, but she was sure to be noticed all the same. She must have been aware of the commotion she was causing. Beneath the palm trees some young boys pretended to be absorbed in play; every few moments they stole a look. Farther along the beach, a group of older boys and men had plainly gathered to watch.

Daphne didn't care. Her head was to one side on the soft wicker basket she used as a pillow. She wore the black sunglasses. I couldn't tell if she was asleep or not. Between her legs on the sand lay a paperback novel, unopened.

"Daphne," I said.

She turned, moving her hand to her forehead.

"Hello, David." She smiled. "Coming swimming?"

"No, not swimming. Actually, I'm here because there have been complaints." She was looking up at me. "You've got to wear your bathing suit."

"Oh, *god*. Here, give me a hand."

She reached forward. Her oiled skin rippled, her hair brushed my shoulder. She picked up the top of her bathing suit from the wicker bag, reached behind her back and clipped it. The boys under the palm trees were still, watching.

"Christ. Let's go," Daphne said.

The sun was low but still hot.

On Tuesday Daphne and Larry moved to the Majestic Hotel where they had taken one of the small cottages near the pool. Daphne could walk out of the door of her villa and through a hedge to the beach. She sunbathed and snorkelled. She was at home in the water and thought nothing of swimming to the reef by herself. She'd made a friend at the hotel, also beautiful. Sometimes they went to the beach together, laughing as they lay in the sun.

I rarely saw Larry and Daphne together after they left the house. I rarely saw them at all. There were more complaints about Daphne at the beach, from older, retired people, as well as from Drover and the villagers.

"She and her fellow had another row last night. Could hear them yelling from the bar," Burnett said.

Larry took to drinking at the Riverside Tavern rather than at the Terrace Bar. You could buy drugs there. One day he came into the bank and cashed traveller's cheques worth $2,000. I had to authorize the transaction myself.

I saw Daphne with another man, a visitor with a radiant white yacht in the harbour. They were sitting at one of the round tables at the Terrace Bar, beneath the coconut palms. There was a black Labrador curled at their feet. The man wore white trousers and no shirt and when he lit his cigarette Daphne reached across the table to brush fallen ash from the black curly hairs of his chest.

"Gives me the creeps," said Healey. We were standing on the government dock. He was over from Nassau for Christmas. He would be taking Daphne and Larry back to Marsh Harbour after New Year's.

We stared across the oily waters of the harbour at the flames of small fires flicking through the trees on the far side. We were caught momentarily in the crossing beam of the lighthouse.

"It'll be worse later, when the drinking starts," he said.

I helped him carry his bag and several bottles of dark rum up to my house and then I left for Drover's service.

The congregation was almost entirely made up of locals. Many were relatives of Drover's, descendants of the small group of families from South Carolina who had originally settled the island. In their voices there was a hint of southern drawl. I saw the man who ran the museum, the lady from the craft shop, the postmaster, Constable MacMahon, Mrs. Rainey who sold fish. I took a seat at the back. Then I noticed Daphne. She was sitting two rows ahead, with Larry and the woman from their hotel. We were almost in darkness; the room was lit only by the candles positioned around the altar. The aroma was dense and sweet.

When Daphne turned I saw the smile on her lips, the sparkle in her eyes. She was wearing a white sundress that fell off one shoulder. In the candlelight her skin was oily gold. Around her neck she wore the sunglasses on their silver cord.

"Stand up for Jesus!" Drover demanded. We rose and sang. The children performed a series of tableaux. We sang again: "Silent Night," then a strange local song, with a kind of chant for the chorus.

Daphne and her friend were amused. I could see their heads bobbing. I could hear their whispers, snatches of words and laughter. Their voices grew louder during the reading of the lesson.

"He has this *dog* on his boat," Daphne said.

The reading ended. Daphne and her friend began to giggle. Larry shifted in his seat, edging away from them.

The sermon opened with the story of the baby in the manger

and the Star of Bethlehem, but soon shifted to themes with which Drover was more at home. He started in a soft voice, the voice we heard in the store, but soon he was speaking with real feeling. It was the high point of his year.

"Why did Jesus come to us? He came, my friends, because we are *sinners*. We are all sinners...."

I could see Daphne doubled over, in an attempt to suppress her mirth, uncontrollable, like a schoolgirl. She tried a cough to cover the laughter, but only drew more attention to herself. Drover's forehead glistened. He spoke of money. He spoke of drugs. He spoke of adultery. He hurled accusations, imprecations. He glared at the back of the church.

"Hypocrisy. Hypocrisy and evil are filling the world. But God will make them pay. God's will be done!"

Daphne's laugh burst forth and filled the hall. I left the service with it still cascading in my ears.

Back at the house I had dinner with Healey and Burnett. We drank the dark rum. All night long we heard the sounds of celebration in the town: the clanking of sticks pulled along the picket fence that lined the Queen's Highway; the clatter of garbage cans rolling down the pavement, the staccato burst of fireworks above the reggae beat from the harbour.

An early story said that Daphne had been taken away and raped by Haitians, deranged refugees who lived in the bush, men lurking in the trees who had seen her on the beach — naked, tall and white. This was the preferred version at the Yacht Club.

Others, in the village, said the white boys with whom she'd been drinking and dancing earlier in the evening were involved.

She'd enticed them and after a night of rum and debauchery had been left on the beach to be carried away by the sea. There had been trouble like this before on Christmas Eve. Whatever had happened, people said she'd had it coming.

The facts were more mundane. After church, Daphne and her friend sat at the hotel bar drinking with Larry. When he went to bed, they joined the dancing at the government pier. They returned to the hotel for a nightcap. That was the last anyone saw of her.

In the morning, Larry assumed Daphne had gone to the beach, but then she hadn't returned for lunch. Because of sharks beyond the reef, there was little chance of the body being found.

That was the official version: that Daphne had drowned while swimming alone. Constable MacMahon told me this himself.

"What about Larry?" I asked him.

"What are you saying?" he said.

"The estranged husband," I said. "Everyone knows they fought. She flirted with other men. He was the one who wanted her to come down to the islands. She hadn't wanted to come. Maybe he was planning something."

"He says he was in their villa all night. We can't prove otherwise."

I told Constable MacMahon about the $2,000 in traveller's cheques. "Perhaps he paid someone down at the Riverside," I added.

"Paid someone for what?"

"To do her in," I said.

"You have a fevered imagination," Constable MacMahon said. "But you're right about one thing. He approached a pair of Colombians last week. We had a tip-off from someone in the Riverside kitchen. Trouble is, those fellows weren't here that night; they were in Miami." He paused to wipe his brow. "Besides, we have no body."

Larry took the ferry across the channel the day after New Year's.

A week later I was in Drover's store. We were alone. Drover went to the back room and returned with a greasy paper bag.

"Maybe you want these." He handed it to me.

I looked in the bag. The sunglasses with the silver straps.

"Where did you get them?"

"Some fishermen found them," he said. "Boys from the church."

"Where did they find them?"

He hesitated for only a moment. "Washed up down the beach somewhere, I guess."

He rang up my groceries and packed them carefully into a white plastic bag.

"God's will, a thing like that," he said, not looking at me. "God's will."

But my version (surely as true as any other) was that Daphne went with the man from the yacht, swam out to meet his boat. I knew she was a strong swimmer. One day I would see her again, lithe and golden on a white beach.

Pigeon Cay, April

Last night I dreamed of distant summers, swimming with Karen at Shadow Lake. Sunset and the orange-yellow light low through the tops of the white pines and oaks, the bay framed by rocky headlands. Smoke rising from a small fire on the beach; hot days, made hotter by our lovemaking. Even though the evenings brought a small breeze, we were in the water constantly....

I understand that, in memory, distant times like those acquire a rose patina. But that's behind me. Now I have Annie. She is my secret life. I kissed her for the first time at the reggae club. The food was terrible, the air foul and smoky, the beer warm, the mood frantic. The music was too loud to be heard when we spoke and I put my hand on her thigh. She turned toward me. Her hands were smooth, her skin cool.

She seems to have put our first meeting at the bank behind her, the scene at the Club. I wonder who is the father of Azalea.

News travels. Burnett has made it clear again that he does not approve, yet the last time he was in Montreal he got drunk and tried to pick up a boy from the mailroom. Made an ass of himself. All the same, I should not be seen consorting with a black woman, he says. It's bad for business.

Showed more of my stories to Tommas. He said, "What are you doing working at a bank? Why are you doing business with drug dealers? It will ruin this place and it will be on your head. Not to mention the waste of your talents." The first time it has been put so directly.

He also asked me if I knew anything about the Hotel Paradiso, about what goes on there, the people who pass through. I know it is run-down, almost derelict. It's isolated, on the lee side of the island, rather than on the picture-perfect ocean side, with the reef, crashing surf and the miles of palm-fringed beaches where most of the other hotels and rental houses are located. The Paradiso is inaccessible by road but has its own pier, stretching far out into the bay. The hotel compound looks like an abandoned U.S. base, something in the Philippines, Guam. There always seem to be piles of garbage burning in the bush behind the main building, acrid smoke rising high in the still air.

Tommas writes mostly poetry, has published widely, is interested in the unwritten history and stories of the islands. He has complex theories about the cultures of place, those that were conquered (his word) by the British, the French, the Spanish. All destructive, but in his view the Spanish were the least so. "Look at Cuba, they allowed the traditions of the African slaves to flourish, kept families and tribes together. The places the British settled and then left are the most damaged, the most rotten. Like Pigeon Cay." Exactly the reverse of what people at the Yacht Club would say; they think they've found a paradise, the best of all possible worlds. Tommas says we're an outpost of the British and now the American empire. I asked him about Delraney, a local grandee with ambitions as a writer. He only sneered.

Annie and I talk about writing too, and what we've read. We talk about seeing our reflections on the page, the patterns. But what if there are no patterns, if there is no reason events unfold in a particular way? I'm writing a story about writing a story, about framing and organizing events, describing real and imaginary people. Part of the series about this place. I am writing to make sense of it all.

Fíve

"We meet at last," said Delraney. He rose from his wicker chair to greet me. He was tall, thin, all smiles and courtly solicitude, although I noticed he hadn't come down to help me at the pier. He would have heard the sound of the outboard. The wind was from the northeast that day and the rage between the gaps was strong. My slicker and hair were soaking wet and I'd damaged the gunwale landing the dinghy in the choppy cross-hatch waves of the inner channel.

"You get the weather here," I said.

"To people like you, it's bad weather. But we're used to it. The sea is why we are here."

He watched me wrestle with my greasy coat. I was not at one with boats.

"My family used to build boats," he said. "A hundred years ago. Boat building, fishing, sisal and sail making, sponging, salvaging the foreign wrecks on the reef. We survived by the sea."

I climbed awkwardly onto the pier. He has already turned toward the house.

"Let me take your coat. Dry yourself and we'll have a glass of rum." He called out in French and a Haitian boy appeared from the kitchen. Delraney gave instructions. When we were alone, he turned and said, "So. You're some kind of writer?"

People were always saying to me, "You must visit Delraney." He lived like a hermit, the only inhabitant of a scraggly island beyond the southern gap, where the Atlantic rollers break through the reef. He was in his late 60s. He rarely came to the village and then only to conduct a class or two at the school beyond the graveyard. Since Independence, the government had introduced to the curriculum something called "Indigenous Arts and Culture," about which the expatriates made cruel jokes. He must have done his banking across the channel, because I rarely saw him in the village on business. He was a member of the Yacht Club, but I'd never seen him at any of our Saturday nights, either.

The boy brought us dark rum and ice, along with a plate of conch fritters. You had to pound the conch to make it tender, then cut the rubbery flesh into tiny pieces, while the creature squirmed.

"The conch is a threatened species," I said.

Delraney's family had been food importers in Nassau and he had made more money in land development. His shelves were filled with well-bound books, though the salt air did them no good. The furnishings in the house were solid wood and polished. Beside the veranda was a large black satellite dish.

"I was saying, they tell me you write," said Delraney. I could see the little magazine with my story in it on the table, almost hidden. "I thought you were a banker," he said.

"Not *just* a banker." At one time I'd wanted to join the

Foreign Service. I was attracted to its melancholy.

"You've heard the joke about the novelist who tells the neurosurgeon he'd like to take up brain surgery," said Delraney, "if only he could find the time?"

Delraney had had some essays and poems in newspapers, a novel (long out of print) and, most recently, a story in a collection paid for and put out by the Ministry of Education.

"Ah, but you're a real writer," I said. I had spotted his novel on the bookshelf — there must have been 10 copies — and I bowed toward them in a show of respect.

Delraney waved his arm in a breezy gesture. "That's nothing."

When he left the room a few moments later, I examined the novel and decided that this was no less than the truth. The book had been published privately in Nassau; the print was photocopied typescript. It appeared to be a memoir. It was very short.

"I'm working on a series of stories now," he said.

"What sort of stories?" I asked.

"About a boy who was raised in the islands, goes away to attend university and remains to make a career. He returns to the islands in late middle age, to try to find peace, but he finds that things have…changed. The stories are to some degree autobiographical."

Then he leaned forward in his chair, changing the subject, "Why is there so much about the Haitians in your stories, drug addicts and so on? Why don't you talk about the real people?"

"The Haitians and smugglers are real," I said.

"Not really," said Delraney

"What about Tommas? He's a Haitian. He's also a poet."

"Tommas is a black workman and a bartender," said Delraney. "He was here cleaning out my cistern last week."

"You never discuss his writing?"

"No," said Delraney.

"I've seen his poems," I said. "They're published in St. Lucia. A thousand miles from here."

I meant that Tommas' work was published in another country, not by the Ministry of Education.

"And the boy who served our drinks?" I said. "He's Haitian."

"I don't deny that they are here. But they come and go, like the tourists. Like you people with the foreign banks. They're refugees. It all depends on what's happening in Haiti, the political situation, what the Americans are up to, whether they can make enough money to go home. But they're not important. You can't see that. Refugees, drug dealers, rich tourists and prostitutes — it's all the same to you."

I thought that the refugees were as important as the rumrunners had been during Prohibition. And I knew that the tourists and drugs were important: I saw the money, week after week. We were at the edge of empire, an American empire; the islands were lapped by genteel corruption.

"What surprises me," said Delraney, "is how much you seem to think you know after a year. You come here with a foreign bank and then you write romantic nonsense about foreigners, palm trees, the sun. I've noticed that palm trees are always on the covers of these books about the south. And yet," he waved dismissively, "you're afraid of the sea."

The last straw. He spoke in a plain voice, but his face had gone dark again; he was angry. We finished our drinks in silence. Delraney rose to get the servant, who shortly returned with refills.

"Tell me," he asked, smiling again, "how do you get a story in a magazine like that anyway?" He pointed to the one on the table. "You have to know the publisher, I suppose?"

I gave him the name of a publisher in Miami who had told me he was interested in tales of the West Indies.

"They never publish us," said Delraney. He'd become a little gloomy. "The people who actually live here, I mean."

On the pier, when I was leaving, he said, "Be careful of the rage."

The rage came when a combination of high tide and gale winds forced the sea through the breaks in the reef and over the sandbars in immense swells. You could be cruising quietly up the leeward channel when suddenly the rage came through and ran you aground. In the 19th century, ships were wrecked that way. The villagers would douse their lights and wait on the dark shore for salvage.

Seeing myself in the story was a shock. It was a small magazine printed in New Providence, on paper like the Yellow Pages, and published irregularly at that. There were poems, essays, short stories and strange line drawings. The story was called "Foreigners," and there was a grotesque picture of an eagle in a frock suit.

Burnett was there too, a rapacious cartoon character, like some rich planter in colonial Malaysia. The bank was identified by name, unfortunately. Someone in the Nassau office had found the story and sent it to Burnett. Burnett came to me soon after.

"We can't have this." He rapped at the photocopy with the back of his hand. "Is this your doing? We simply can't have this. Worst possible thing."

Healey was depicted as a drunken playboy. I recognized him at once. There were the idle racists at the Yacht Club, the wealthy expatriates at North Point, the tourists on charter yachts corrupting the young by buying drugs in the back room of the Riverside Tavern, trying to lure the girls below.

Suffusing it all was an air of purity in which lived the

disappointed exile, the native son who had left the islands and returned as a man only to find corruption and disappointment.

I assured Burnett there would be no reverberations; no one with money read this kind of thing. This was the truth. The story came and went without a ripple. Members of the Yacht Club were ignorant of the whole affair. Burnett would never mention it to them and neither would I.

"The Wrecker," or "The Wreckers"? I debated over the title of my own story and finally decided on the plural. It was only Delraney I was after and I thought this would be less obvious. It would be about a man who destroys something by trying to cling to a crumbling past. The historical parallels would be to incidents that had occurred on the island in 1863, when the villagers had refused to supply workers building the lighthouse with food and water and had sabotaged the boat bringing building supplies from the mainland. The coming of the light-house ended the livelihood of the wreckers. In the end, of course, it was the lighthouse that enabled the island to enter the world of trade, illicit or not. On a clear night you can see the wink of the lighthouse for 30 miles.

A few weeks later I went to visit Delraney for the second time. The winter fronts had gone and the heat of summer had yet to begin. The breeze across the water was warm and intoxicating. The green sea was clear.

Delraney was there to greet me at the pier. He led me up the cinder path. We sat on the eastern veranda facing the ocean.

"Rum?" said Delraney. He poured it from a bottle on the table just inside the living room door.

"Where is the boy?" I asked.

"Gone back to Haiti. I gave him the fare. His grandmother died and the family inherited a bit of land somewhere in the hills. He went back to help his father and uncles run the farm."

He brought me my glass. There were no conch fritters.

"To what do I owe this pleasure?" He seemed not unhappy to see me, perhaps a little bored.

"Business, actually, not pleasure. I saw your story," I said. "Congratulations."

"Yes. I owe you thanks for that. The fellow in Miami you mentioned, he took the story immediately."

"You'll do more?" I said. "A series?"

"Perhaps. Perhaps not. I'm becoming an old man. I came back here to live, not to gain a reputation."

"What about my reputation?"

"I wish you well."

"About the bank and the expatriates in your story, do you think that's the truth? About me, Burnett and the others?"

"It's just a story. Fiction. You're simply here among us, aren't you, like the Haitians, those drug runners." He turned and smiled.

Walking back to the pier, I noticed scaffolding behind the house and some kind of wooden structure, half completed.

"My latest project," said Delraney, in answer to my gaze. "I'm building a tower."

"Why?"

"So that I can see farther."

Gregor Robinson

In the early afternoon the wind rose and there was a warning over the weather channel. Broken clouds raced across the sky. At five o'clock, at Drover's store, I heard about the wreck. You could see it from the ridged hump of land in the middle of the island, a sleek cabin cruiser, wallowing on its beam-end on the reef near the southern gap. It had been in the open Atlantic, no doubt to avoid notice, and had attempted to come back behind the islands when the wind rose.

A small crowd gathered. We watched the two men from the cruiser as they found their way ashore in the dinghy; the sea inside the reef remained almost calm. I recognized them as customers of the bank, probably small-time dealers.

As always, the silhouettes of the palms in the wind played against the blue sky. An airplane, glittering like a toy, circled before making its final descent to the airport across the channel.

Pigeon Cay, June

"Put not your trust in money, but your money in trust." That's what Mrs. Holborne says, quoting Oliver Wendell Holmes. Fine for her to say; she has plenty. I know.

Once, several years ago, I was travelling in northern India not long after there had been a war. Only a border skirmish, really, but for a few weeks we weren't allowed to travel farther north. I soon ran out of cash and took a job working in a tourist café, next to a government hostel. The ceiling and walls of the café were blankets and carpets hung from a rough wooden frame. I came in to work in the evenings. The hills above the village were red from the sunset and also, I imagined, from the blood of the soldiers who had been killed there a few weeks before. Our customers were mostly young people — English, Australians, Swedes, Germans — travelling through the East with their backpacks. Some were spiritual seekers, trekkers in search of purgatory. Others were lost to drugs.

They concealed their cash, traveller's cheques, passports, airline tickets and other valuables in all sorts of hiding places: beneath the insoles of their shoes, in silk money belts, sewn into the lining of their backpacks, stuffed into deodorant sticks, in bras and underwear. We knew them all. Sareesh would tell us about new ones as the hostel staff discovered them. One time he said to me, "Sir, that short hirsute gentleman with the stinky cigarettes, he is keeping his hashish bandaged to his scrotum. Oh yes, sir!"

More than I wanted to know. We who served knew everything. So it is here. My job at the bank has given me more knowledge about these people, this place, than I ever wanted. Other people's business. It is becoming impossible to ignore what we are doing here. We *must* all know — Burnett, Healey, the people in Nassau, in Montreal — but we say nothing.

Now there is talk of a casino at the resort across the channel, because there is no legal gambling within a hundred of miles of Pigeon Cay. They allow illegal gambling down at the Goombay Bar, which Annie manages, and she gets a small percentage for looking the other way. This is what she brings to the bank every week, not drug money as Healey had thought. She doesn't approve of the gambling, doesn't like the people it attracts. Still, she makes much better money than the illegal domestics and hotel workers here and without resorting to drugs or prostitution. If the casino opens across the channel, she'll be out of work; she'll never be able to get her papers and leave the islands. And neither will Azalea.

The conventional wisdom is that a casino would be a shot in the arm, that there would be positive ripple effects even in Pigeon Cay. But it will also ruin the place: mass tourism and cruising ships.

The Norwegians who run the Hotel Paradiso have asked for a revolving line of credit. Both Healey and Burnett said we could more or less dispense with the usual due diligence, so the arrangement has been approved.

My latest guest has departed. What people describe as "a character," and not without a certain charm, but I am relieved all the same. She complained about the food, but ate me out of house and home. Her son was a mental case, caused nothing but trouble. Also, it was impossible to have Annie over while the two of them were here.

Annie has started sending me notes, sometimes two or three a day, delivered by one of the boys from the Goombay kitchen. Love letters. Healey has issued a warning; he says she is developing expectations. And I am not the first. Azalea's father was a Canadian lawyer, working in the islands three or four days a month. He was here on behalf of the bank, back when we were first expanding in the Caribbean. They were to be married. So Healey tells me.

Six

A circular appeared: "Music and High Tea at the Palm Court of the Majestic Hotel." Madame Grumbacher was referring to the windowless lobby, three steps below ground level, which also served as the hotel bar and was home to the village dart league. The reception desk would be obscured by a Chinese screen. The bottles behind the bar would be discreet, the yellow bulb that illuminated them unscrewed. Potted plants were to be placed in front of the poolroom door. But why a Palm Court, when all around actual palm trees were swaying in the warm sea breezes?

"Have you ever been to Vienna?" asked Madame Grumbacher. "Or Budapest? Perhaps Saint Mark's, in *Venezia*? All the best hotels have Palm Courts."

And who would prefer to take tea in a gloomy hotel when you could step across the road to the Terrace Bar and have a Beck's or a Goombay Smash under the immense sky?

"English people. Europeans. We are getting a better class of clientele. Plus, we will also offer rum."

"And who will supply the music?"

"A very refined lady. From Massachusetts." Madame

Grumbacher leaned toward me. "Mr. Rennison, you can have a guest at your house, yes?"

"No. Absolutely not."

"A distinguished musician. It will be a surprise for the people of the village."

"It will be a surprise for me."

"She has appeared with the New Bedford Ensemble, only last month!" Madame Grumbacher stood, triumphant, resuming her full height and her normal booming voice. She put my beer on the table. "She will be our first performer. Sunday afternoon. You will be there."

"There must be some mistake."

But there was no mistake. Healey came into the bank after lunch to tell me that a Mrs. Arbuthnot would be coming to stay.

"Why can't she stay at the Majestic? Or the Inn. Or at the Hotel Paradiso?"

"The rooms in the Majestic smell," said Healey. "The Inn is expensive. The Hotel Paradiso is disreputable. Mrs. Arbuthnot is a musician, genteel."

I suggested renting a house, but there was no time for that; she would be arriving any minute.

"Another thing," said Healey. "Mrs. Arbuthnot knows Burnett. He arranged the whole thing."

She arrived the next day, a Monday. I was lunching alone on my terrace overlooking the harbour. An immense straw hat came along the top of the hedge. Then two peacock feathers.

"Mr. Rennison, you're eating lunch!" She had an East Coast accent, accusatory, accustomed to being paid attention. "I went to the bank first, naturally, but it was closed. Nice hours you keep!"

I moved my chair back from the table. Mrs. Arbuthnot put her hands to her ears (I would learn that the sound of furniture scraping on stone was one of the many that bothered her). I commented on her immense earrings: lime-green elephants.

"Yes," she said, "and they shine in the dark."

I asked if she had had lunch.

"I don't want to impose. Really." She picked up a chair and moved it to the table.

"Punch?" I picked up my own glass for a refill.

"That would be lovely," said Mrs. Arbuthnot. "I don't think there was any rum in the last one."

"Your last one?"

"At the hotel. I stopped to ask where you lived. This is awfully kind of you, having me on such short notice. I am touring the islands, giving concerts where I can, arranging my schedule as I go. It's all very difficult."

"A sort of cultural ambassador."

"That is how I think of myself."

She helped herself to a second spiny lobster tail, the one I'd been planning to save for dinner. She smacked as she ate. When I brought her the drink she favoured me with a smile, the cheerful look associated with the round faces of the demented; framed, in her case, by a blonde Dutchboy cut and eye shadow applied with lunatic abandon. She was about 60.

A plane flew overhead. "Why is that plane circling?" said Mrs. Arbuthnot, not looking up. "Listen how he throttles down. Having a look at us, I'd say. Cessna 120. Same as mine. Wonder where he came from? Wasn't at the airport when we landed."

Burnett's voice crackled over the radiophone. I excused myself, went inside to take the call.

"Woman coming to stay — she there yet?" said Burnett. "Awfully sorry."

I told Burnett that he'd hear from me later because just then I realized I had more company. A second voice outside: low, male, sibilant. I picked up the dessert (ice cream and papaya) and pushed the screen door open with my hip. There was now a pile of luggage on the terrace and sitting not at the table but on the wooden bench in the shade by the wall was a man of 30, at most. He was pale, thin, slightly stooped. He held in his lap a hissing cassette machine. The red light was on; he was recording.

"My son," said Mrs. Arbuthnot. "Lloyd, say hello."

" 'Lo." The fellow stared at me like a dead fish.

"Lloyd is taping my concerts," said Mrs. Arbuthnot. "He is 'into' electronics. He is also my radio man and navigator."

After Mrs. Arbuthnot and Lloyd had taken their things to their rooms, I urged them to walk across the island to see the museum and the old cholera cemetery. Sometimes a human bone turned up in the sand — always gratifyingly startling to visitors.

I cleaned the kitchen and checked the bedrooms. Mrs. Arbuthnot's suitcases were half unpacked on one of the twin beds. On the night table were books, brushes, creams, perfumes and other toiletries.

But in Lloyd's room there was no evidence of human visitation: nothing on the floor, on the beds, or on the bureau. I opened the top drawer. There was his clothing, orderly and packed tight, even his shoes.

I heard footfalls behind me, a doe walking on moss.

"See anything you like?" Lloyd stood behind me, his head through the doorway.

I cleared my throat. "Just making sure you have towels."

"The towels are behind the door." Lloyd pointed. He was much younger than I, but his movements were of someone much older. His gestures reminded me of Ichabod Crane.

I strode past him into the hall. Lloyd followed, hands behind back. I said, "Here we have the bathroom."

"Mineral oil in the medicine chest," said Lloyd. "If you're constipated, you should use fruits and natural fibre."

"I am not constipated," I replied icily. "The mineral oil was here when I rented the house." The tour continued into the living room.

"See you like Glenn Gould. I do, too." He'd been here two hours yet he'd examined the medicine chest and my cassettes. It occurred to me that his interest in electronics was just the tip of the iceberg. I'd read about people like Lloyd. They lived in rooms by themselves. They had binoculars. They kept dossiers. They had a fondness for ice picks. One day, they went berserk.

"I thought you were going to the beach," I said.

"I've been to the beach," said Lloyd. "Came back to check on my equipment. Just as well. Mother's cello has arrived."

"Cello?" I thought she was a pianist.

"Couldn't fit in the taxi, had to get a van. There's a man here, wants us to go down to the harbour and pick it up."

We borrowed Drover's jitney, which he used for picking up vegetables and meat from the freight boat, and drove down to the pier. The cello wasn't heavy so much as awkward; we finally secured it with ropes to the top of the jitney. The water-taxi operator stood waiting. Lloyd shrugged and gave me a blank look, so I told the man to put it on my account.

At dinner that night Mrs. Arbuthnot said, "I owe you money for the water taxi." She said there would be a letter of credit coming from Massachusetts; we would settle later.

My visitors were soon well known in the village. Mrs. Arbuthnot visited every gimcrack souvenir shop, talking, buying and delivering circulars about the concert. Lloyd's appearances were more peculiar. He said little, he dressed sombrely and he went farther afield. The second day, he rose early and walked the length of the island. The third, he borrowed a rowboat from the hotel and explored the coves, the hurricane hole and the mangrove swamps on the lee side.

Wherever he went, he carried one of his tape recorders. He had several small cassette players and a large machine with dials and fluttering needles. Madame Grumbacher told me that he spent several afternoons at the indoor bar of the Majestic (the new Palm Court). He was the only person there besides the dart players. The red light of his tape recorder glowed in the gloom. He had a boom mike.

"What do you think you're doing?" one of the men in the dart league had asked.

"Just testing," said Lloyd. He stared the man down. "For the concert."

At the Terrace Bar, he sat on the far side wearing earphones, the boom mike aimed across the pool toward the thatched hut. It made people edgy. He even ventured into the Riverside, ordered colas — Lloyd did not drink alcohol — and sat with a recorder in his pocket. The room was silent but for the whir of the cassette player and the click of the cues, until the bartender told Lloyd to shut the recorder off or have it shoved down his throat.

Ti-Paul from the ferry came into the bank expressly to tell me about this incident. "That man you got staying with you, he the police?"

"Does he look it?" I asked.

"Yeah, well, he better be careful. The boys at the Riverside, they got bad nerves. He spooks them."

"Tell them he's a tourist, good for business."

Mrs. Arbuthnot was rarely in the house; when she wasn't out

"getting to know the villagers — so colourful," she was at the Methodist Chapel where Madame Grumbacher had arranged for her to rehearse. But Lloyd was in and out like a wraith. He would materialize in the kitchen, on the terrace, in the living room, his tape recorders whirring, then vanish.

Friday was my busiest day and I was at the bank by eight o'clock. The restaurants, the merchants, the visitors in yachts — everyone needed cash for the weekend. Traffic in my bathroom was heavy. Mrs. Arbuthnot's ablutions took almost an hour, including a bath, a shampoo, drying her hair with a blower that made the lights fade and the toaster pop.

"Mr. Rennison!" Winnie said, bursting in the side door of the bank. Her hair was wild.

"What is it?" I said.

She stared at me, goggle-eyed. I thought I might have to go around the desk and slap her. Suddenly she shouted: "Fire! Fire!"

"What? Here?"

"Riverside Tavern!" she said. "The boathouse!"

I noticed something sweet and oddly familiar in the morning air. I followed Winnie out as the fire bell rang. Constable MacMahon was pulling the rope, rousing the volunteers. But when they went to start the truck, the battery was missing (suspicious, people said later). But there would have been little chance of putting out the fire anyway; the Riverside boathouse was built on piers about 15 yards out in the lagoon. The catwalk had burned by the time Winnie and I arrived and the flames were dying down. Thick smoke lay over the harbour. A crowd had gathered along the path.

"*Sheee-it*! Smell it, man," said Vero, the bartender from the

Majestic. He made a show of inhaling, rolled his eyes. Marijuana smoke filled the air. Out in the harbour I saw Schindler, owner of the Riverside, standing on the deck of his cruiser. He wore a long white dressing gown and dark glasses. He stood perfectly still. He did not look concerned.

With a crash and a hiss, the floor of the boathouse fell into the harbour. Wild applause from the crowd.

When I returned to the bank after lunch there was a cardboard box on my desk — a foot and a half long, maybe a foot wide and a foot high, sealed with thick tape.

"Winnie, what is this?"

"Mr. Schindler's boat boy brought it in for safekeeping. Said you'd know."

But I didn't know. I picked the package up. At least 15 pounds. We had a safe large enough to hold cash for the day, occasionally overnight, and perhaps a few documents.

"Winnie, this parcel will never fit into our safe. You shouldn't have accepted it." She shrugged her shoulders. A copy of the receipt she had given Schindler lay on my desk.

"He's a customer, Mr. Rennison. You always say, treat the customers nice. The customer is always right. That's what you always say, Mr. Rennison. You do."

I heard the sound of the Land Rover on the harbour road. An unexpected visit. Burnett was sweating when he came in, although his silver hair remained firmly in place. I stood, prepared to accompany him across the road for a glass of rum. But there were no pleasantries. He waved me back to my chair with a flutter of the handkerchief he used to wipe his brow.

He said, "You've noticed these bloody airplanes."

"Airplanes?"

"Bloody gnats circling the island. Spotter planes. Now the police are coming. A bloody swoop."

We had two kinds of drugs on Pigeon Cay. Bales of marijuana came from Jamaica and Mexico for local use and for shipment elsewhere. And cocaine. According to Healey, both the cartels and the U.S. government were supposed to have informants on Pigeon Cay. The Americans believed that fishermen picked up packages, which were dropped by air or ship along the lee side of the island, down past the sound. The drugs were transferred to speedboats, which made the runs to Miami under cover of darkness. You could sometimes hear the rumble of engines at night. From time to time the police made sweeps of the islands looking for trawlers, speedboats, anything they could find.

"Explains the fire," I said.

"Fire?"

"The boathouse of the Riverside burned down this morning."

"Ah. Actually, Schindler was out to see me last night," said Burnett. "Don't like the fellow. Still…."

"Absolutely," I said. "A client."

"Wants a favour of some kind. Sending him along to see you."

Of course. Everybody was on the take, from the Prime Minister down. Burnett wouldn't want to know about the favour. By then I knew I'd already done it.

I called Healey, asked him to come over later. When he arrived, I pointed to the package on the kitchen table. "From Schindler. He wants me to put this in the safe."

"Cocaine? What about Burnett?" said Healey.

"You know Burnett. See no evil, hear no evil."

"So, why don't you put it in the safe?"

"Because it won't fit unless we open it, if then. And if we open it, we know what it is."

"I see your point," said Healey. "Let's keep the package under your bed for now. We don't know for sure the sweep will happen."

Gregor Robinson

Saturday night I joined Healey, Burnett and Tom Hargreaves at the Snug Bar. The conversation turned to the topic of our visitors. Hargreaves said that some of the villagers shared the view that Mrs. Arbuthnot should stop buying. The shopkeepers had been giving her credit on the strength of her connection with the bank, but the bills were mounting and they were becoming concerned.

"Stretching a point to call her a friend," said Burnett. "Had a letter from a chap in Boston. Good cause and so forth. Said why not, we'd put her up."

" 'We' meaning me," I said. "And there's two of them."

"Didn't know anything about the son," said Burnett.

"What about those tape recorders?" said Healey. "He's been all over the island. They think he's looking for drop sites. They think he's with the police."

"Is that possible?" said Burnett.

The police arrived on Sunday, the same day as the concert.

"They're going house to house," said Lloyd, back from his early-morning walk. He was more animated than I had ever seen him.

"Impossible," I said. "That would be illegal. They would need search warrants and so on."

But when I stopped in at Drover's to pick up the Miami papers, I saw them, a group of men in shiny black shoes and synthetic jackets coming up the Queen's Highway from the pier. They wore dark sunglasses. You weren't supposed to catch their eye, but how could you tell? I saw another group, in uniforms, heading out along the road to North Point in a jeep.

Back at my house, I rushed to the bedroom and hauled the package out. The cistern. I would suspend the box on a rope from the roof of the tank. I grabbed the package and ran into the garden. The trapdoor to the cistern had two metal handles, but the door was concrete; it would require a tractor to move it. A plane swooped in low from the west. I stooped over the package, imagining that they might be able to spot it from the air. When the plane was out of sight I carried the box back into the house, trying to conceal it under my shirt. Mrs. Arbuthnot and Lloyd were standing by the window. They had evidently watched my entire performance.

"Is this the contraband?" said Mrs. Arbuthnot.

"Contraband? What do you mean?"

"Lloyd's tape recorder." Lloyd held up a tiny microphone. "Under the chesterfield."

I gaped at them.

"I must say, I am disappointed, Mr. Rennison. Very disappointed. I'd have thought you would go straight to the police. In my opinion drugs are a scourge. You should visit certain parts of Boston, or New Haven."

"But, you don't think, if you heard on the tape recorder...."

She held up her hand to stop me. Then she pointed at the box (I saw where Lloyd had learned the gesture), an Old Testament prophet. "So what are you doing? Trying to hide the package?"

A brief pause. Mrs. Arbuthnot said, "Tell you what. Let's put it in the cello case."

"How on earth? That would mean opening the package...."

"Let us not be hypocrites, Mr. Rennison. Lloyd will look after it."

I busied myself with the breakfast. Lloyd came out of the bedroom 20 minutes later, lugging the cello case.

"Had to remove the extra strings," he said, "the tool kit, the resin, empty all the compartments. But it's all in there." He tapped the case with the flat of his hand. "Fifteen little bags, like packages of icing sugar."

I interrupted him. "Yes, certainly, all right then. How about another cup of coffee, some waffles?"

The police reached our end of the village after lunch, a fat sergeant and four men in uniform, the same group from the jeep I'd seen in the morning. Two of the men were smoking cigars.

"Excuse me, sir, a few questions. Mind if the lads have a look around while we talk?" He was English. The soldiers were black.

"You have a search warrant?"

The sergeant removed his hat and scratched his head. He looked tired. "No. No, sir, that we don't. But the drug squad, they do. Every house in the village. They're concentrating on the obvious places, the bars, the boathouses up the swamp. Very thorough, they are. Look everywhere, tear up the floors, piss in the cistern. Don't miss a trick. And good with their hands, if you take my meaning. Shall I get them?"

I stood to let the men pass. They glanced in the cupboards, under the beds. Lloyd hovered in the background.

"Lovely view," said the sergeant, gazing out the double doors to the terrace. "You hear things at night? See boats entering the harbour, like?"

"No," I lied.

The sergeant turned to the cello case leaning against the wall. "What's this, then?"

"A cello," I rasped. Then, regaining my composure, "It belongs to my houseguest, the distinguished American cellist, Alexandra Amelia Arbuthnot. No doubt you have heard her. She is on tour. She is giving a concert at the Majestic Hotel this evening."

"Right, let's have a look." He motioned to one of the soldiers. I watched frozen, horrified.

The door of the bathroom opened. Mrs. Arbuthnot emerged in a cloud of steam. She wore a long silk dressing gown, which clung to her robust figure. Her hair hung wet about her head as though she were a sea goddess. She was armed with the hair dryer. She said. "Do not touch that case."

"Eh?" said the sergeant.

"The instrument inside that case is 200 years old. It is extremely delicate. If the damp sea air touches it, untold damage will result. My tour will be in ruins. I am a guest of your government. I shall hold you responsible." She returned to the bathroom and shut the door.

The sergeant stared after her for a moment. Then he said, "Right then, we're on our way. Come along, lads."

We passed the other group of police as we carried the cello from my house to the hotel later that afternoon.

"Tell me," I said to Mrs. Arbuthnot, "are you really a guest of the government?"

"In a manner of speaking. Their representative stamped my passport. By the way, you needn't wait for us after the concert. There's going to be a small reception. Madame Grumbacher is giving us dinner."

To Madame Grumbacher's credit, the Palm Court looked quite believable. The chesterfields and armchairs had been replaced with round tables and folding chairs. Footlights had been borrowed from the Methodist Church Drama Club. The stage was set up in the corner, with an upright piano and a chair and music stand for Mrs. Arbuthnot. Behind the piano were enormous potted palms. There were seats for perhaps 75 in the room and all were taken. Another 10 or 15 people stood at the bar.

Lloyd fussed about, setting up his machines. Then he vanished.

The police arrived halfway through the concert, five of them, the ones in plain clothes and dark glasses. They stood at the back and surveyed the crowd. A murmuring and shuffling of chairs as people turned. Mrs. Arbuthnot's cello case lay closed on the floor beneath the piano. After another 15 minutes the police left, clumping along the wooden floor in counterpoint to "Lara's Theme."

After the concert, I returned home and had dinner by myself, one of the casseroles that Burnett's housekeeper, Mrs. Hamish, prepared for me twice weekly. I opened a bottle of wine and took my plate onto the terrace. It was a warm night and windless; the putrid smell of the mangrove swamp wafted across the harbour. Around eleven o'clock, two lumbering police boats headed out toward the channel. The sweep was over. In the distance I heard the engine of a small plane.

I was awakened in darkness. Something jarred the house. I heard shouting. Beating against the walls; any minute they seemed likely to hit a window. I grabbed my robe from the hook. About 15 men were gathered in the blackness of the garden. I recognized a few from the Riverside. There was the smell of liquor. I saw the flash of a pool cues. Someone said, "Where's the spook, boss?"

There had been several arrests that day among the smaller dealers who hung around Annie's and the Riverside Tavern. Now the police were gone and they wanted their revenge.

"It's four in the morning. Come back tomorrow. You want me to call MacMahon?" This was a hollow threat and they knew it. I heard a commotion behind me; some of the men had entered the house by forcing the terrace doors. I turned and the others swarmed past me. The bedroom lights were switched on.

But there was no one there. Madame Grumbacher had spirited them away. Lloyd must have come back during the concert and taken their luggage. Their flight only confirmed the belief that Lloyd had been undercover, that he'd brought the police. But now he was gone and they were mollified.

Schindler was not. His voice came over the radio first thing in the morning, squawking my name before I'd finished shaving. I picked an open channel.

"You're phoning about your documents?" I said.

"My documents?"

"The package. I assumed it was documents, the way it was sealed."

"Documents? That is what you assumed?"

"That is what I assumed. Were they important documents?"

"Important? Yes. They were important documents, Mr. Rennison. They were vitally important."

"I'm sorry to hear that. The package wouldn't fit into the safe at the bank, as I'm sure you must have known, so I brought it home with me. Must have got mixed up with my guests' luggage."

"Mixed up?"

"The taxi driver must have loaded it in the van. I presume they took the package with them."

Silence. As in all the out islands, it was a citizen's band system. Anyone could listen in and people often did.

Finally he said, "Perhaps they will remember at the airport." A pause. "They may be searched."

"Perhaps. But she was travelling in her own plane."

"How convenient."

"Yes. You should make a list of those documents, for the authorities. In the meantime, I'll let you know if I hear anything."

I did hear something, two days later: a package in the mail with a letter attached:

Dear Mr. Rennison,

A note to thank you for your hospitality. I'm sorry we weren't able to say goodbye in person, but we thought it best to leave at once, you understand. Enclosed, tapes of the concert. Also Lloyd's other tapes. Our flight was uneventful, except that the cargo door unexpectedly flew open mid air, dispersing my cello case into the sea. A freak accident. Luckily, the cello was not in the case at the time. Call if you are ever in Great Barrington.

Sincerely, A. Arbuthnot.

Schindler wasn't the only one to take a loss. Drover came to see me, wanted payment for an account of about $200. "She said it was all right, you'd look after it." There were similar stories from Vero at the hotel, the Inn, where Mrs. Arbuthnot had taken Burnett and others for elaborate dinners, from the lady who ran the hat and dress shop, from others. The total came to over $1,000. And then there was a call from the airport: $300 for airplane fuel. I paid the bills out of my own pocket. I owed her that.

Pigeon Cay, September

The bank is busier than ever. So much money is coming in that Healey and I have found it prudent to take the cash out of the vault twice a week, sometimes three times, and ferry it across the channel in the MacKee. Healey occasionally stays over, using the trips to visit tourist nightclubs and low-end bars. Last night, he wound up with a girl only 18 years old. Two years older than Azalea.

Under the rear deck of the MacKee we now keep a Mini M-14. The magazine holds 32 bullets. Half of them are soft-headed for human targets and half are armour piercing, to stop boats. The bullets are loaded in alternating sequence. My job is to unwrap the M-14 — we keep it in the safe, swaddled in oily rags — and take it down to the harbour every Monday and Thursday in one of the canvas cash bags.

Smugglers are also taking advantage of the increased cash flow in the islands, seizing cruisers and motor yachts, which they use for single runs to Florida and then abandon in swamps and deserted coves. The government has gone so far as to risk issuing a warning to tourists: no landing at secluded beaches; no approaching strange boats; above all, no unnecessary disturbances — if you leave the smugglers alone, they will leave you alone (as though they were shy woodland creatures). Last night Burnett made some mention of U.S. agents operating in the area. He says they may have informants here. (Possible story?) He looked at me pointedly; it was another of his veiled warnings. We appear to be siding with our dubious customers on these matters: if they're worried about the U.S. government, then so is the bank.

Got a letter from Ed Holder in connection with a story he's working on. He's based in Havana, covering Latin America for several U.S. and Canadian papers. Perhaps he's looking into the matters to which Burnett alluded.

As for my own writing, I've been experimenting lately with techniques of suspense, the use of different kinds of language, unreliable narrators. Tommas says the voice in some of the stories I've shown him is too detached. He shuns technique in favour of the political, wants to discuss narrative in terms of supporting or undermining "existing power structures." He says it's bad enough I'm working for the forces of international capitalism and globalization, do I also have to write stories that take the side of racists or feature older white men exploiting young black women? (Was he also alluding to Annie and me?) Exactly the reverse, I say, I am focusing attention on the situation and, besides, my characters get their just desserts. But Tommas says he will do the interpreting. Healey says it's people like Tommas, Ti-Paul, the Cuban fellow Eduardo, who tried to blow up the bank in New Providence, who are the real threat.

Last night A. came to the house just after midnight, having ridden all the way from the other end of the island on her bicycle, a heavy British contraption that does not suffer bumps well. Increasingly, she arrives bearing gifts: fresh limes and papayas, high-proof Jamaican rum, foreign magazines. Later, she fell asleep, damp against my body. I am growing accustomed to her gifts and indulgences, our nights together, the scent of soap and dust that lingers on her skin. She asked me again about going to the mainland, about our future, even having children. But I don't like to think about the future.

I've been in Pigeon Cay almost a year and a half now. Soon I'll be battening down the shutters for hurricane season.

Seven

The Russian satellite turned me into a blackmailer. When the men from Washington came with their plastic identity cards and dark suits, I had no choice. For a few weeks the satellite had been a shot in the arm for the whole island: a pearl from heaven. And by remaining quiet about what I knew, I saved Vero's life.

"She was ketch-rigged, 44 feet," Tom Hargreaves said. "We were taking her from the Cape to Bermuda for the winter. It was late in the year for that kind of crossing — the middle of November, weather unreliable — but her owner was a friend of mine in the…Service. I agreed as a favour. My son was along with his girl, as was the owner's friend, a banker. He was supposed to be doing some work for us, on back-to-back loans, laundering operations, flight capital, that sort of thing. More coffee?" He reached across for the pot on the glass table.

We were sitting on the terrace of Hargreaves' house, a low villa nestled below the ridge on the Atlantic side of the island. The breeze was gentle and warm and the ocean broke lazily on the white sand below.

"No, thanks," I said.

Mary came out of the house and fussed with the pot as

though she were the maid. She was solicitous, nervous.

"The weather hit toward the end of the second day. Real Atlantic weather, the worst I'd ever seen," said Tom.

"Wind out of the northeast. Got up to 40 knots. Managed to get the main down. Continued under the mizzen reefed and a headsail. The stays held and we kept her steady though none of us felt at all well. We each did a watch, then went straight to bed. My boy's girl kept things neat below, did the cooking. Then the electricity went. We had an auxiliary radio, but nothing else: no lights, no heat, motor wouldn't turn over. The banker fellow stayed below for good. Too sick, he said, couldn't help with anything. Of course he had the aft cabin so the rest of us took turns in the saloon, snatching rest where we could. He didn't recover until we were safe in the harbour at Hamilton. Then he was fine, off golfing with friends, drinking; we hardly saw him."

Hargreaves paused to let the enormity of the outrage sink in.

"Terrible thing, a poor sailor," said Burnett.

"Worse than that. Turned out the fellow had been selling secrets to the Russians," said Hargreaves. "He was on his way out of the country when he signed on with us. Plans had been made. Bermuda, then a boat to Cuba, something like that. I must say, I wasn't surprised. You sail with a fellow, you see his true colours. He ended up in jail."

"You do much sailing now?" I asked.

There was a horrible silence. Burnett looked down at his feet. Hargreaves looked out to sea. I thought maybe he hadn't heard me and was about to repeat the question when Burnett slapped the arms of his chair.

"Well, Tom, we must be off. People to see. Thanks for the coffee. You know where you can find David if you want to talk details," said Burnett, gesturing in my direction. "He knows all the tax arrangements down here. Very convenient. Do all my banking in the village now. You should, too."

"Right," said Hargreaves.

We walked through the house to the front door. The main room was obsessively neat, *National Geographic*s and yachting magazines at right angles on glass table tops. There were framed antique maps on the walls, a barometer, nautical curios and ship's instruments. In a small room to the side was a table set up with two-way radio equipment.

Mary came out of the kitchen and walked us through the garden. At the front gate she turned to me and said, "Thank you for coming."

"It was my pleasure." I said, smiling.

She shook my hand quickly and lightly by the fingertips, then interlaced her fingers neatly in front of her, to keep them still.

"Drop by again. Tom needs the company."

"What was all that about?" I said to Burnett, as we strolled along the road back to the village.

"Tom used to be a great sailor. Cape Cod, regattas, all that. Then a couple of years ago, he had some accident on an Atlantic crossing. Lost his nerve. He hasn't set foot on his sloop in the harbour for two years. He'll get over it," said Burnett. "But it is best not to talk about it. Anyway, stay in his good book. He knows people and he's legit."

People in the bank's head office were getting nervous: some of the other offshore branches were getting a reputation as havens for illegal funds.

"So where does it come from?" I said. "His money?"

"Family," said Burnett. "Old money."

"The best kind," I said.

Tom Hargreaves' forebears had been friendly with presidents, ambassadors, the Rockefellers. He'd retired early after a career in the Foreign Service.

"They say round here it had something to with government intelligence," said Burnett. "A spy."

Sometimes I saw Tom at the Terrace Bar of the Majestic, bored and out of place in that *déclassé* setting. It never failed, there was always a passing reference to his sleuthing, "Better watch what you say. We have the CIA here," followed by a wink at old Tom, who would smile and hoist his bourbon.

Despite these social connections, I never saw Tom professionally. At the bank Winnie occasionally cashed a traveller's cheque for Mary, nothing more. When I ran into Tom socially he made jokes about how the bank, how *we*, were taking money out of the country and lending it in Montreal and New York to western oil men. Exactly what we were doing, of course. Still, it didn't make us fast friends.

Like a ship, our island was self-contained and everyone heard soon enough what was going on. The village was the nerve centre, news flowed like an electric current: from the government dock when the ferry came in; from Drover's store where the villagers and the expatriates did their shopping; from the Riverside Tavern and the Terrace Bar. The people who lived farther away — at the end of North Point, or toward Tilloo Cay, or on a more remote island — would hear the news when they came to the Yacht Club Saturday nights. The refugees from Haiti and Cuba who lived in the bush had their own network, of which we knew little.

"A wreck," Winnie said, "washed up on the beach. Vero found it this morning." That was the earliest version. It must have been within an hour or two of Vero having found the thing.

Vero was a boy from one of the families that had been on Pigeon Cay for 200 years. They lived at the far end of the island.

He usually came to the village on an old bicycle, walking part of the way, using trails through the bush. He knew what was going on in the Haitian settlements. One time he asked if I could speak Spanish, said he wanted to talk with some of the Cuban refugees. He was a regular source of information at the Terrace Bar.

"A piece of metal. That's all it is," Burnett told me. It was Friday and he had come into town, as was his custom, for his mail, his banking and a couple of drinks at the hotel.

"Have you seen it?" I asked.

"No. One of the fellows working on my tennis court told me. Friend of Vero's."

Vero worked at the bar Saturdays; it was their busiest time. He was pounding conch for the fritters in the little kitchen at the rear and helping serve mixed drinks and beer at the thatched hut by the swimming pool when I stopped by.

He'd been riding his bike in the scrubby growth above the beach when he came across it. He found it high up in the grass, beyond the line of debris washed in by the surf at high tide.

"It could have been thrown up in the spring," I said, "or even last year."

"Too shiny for that, man. Wasn't old enough. And it wasn't there before. I know 'cause I would have seen it. You got to go see for yourself."

Vero's personal theory was that the piece of metal had fallen from the sky.

"From a plane," he said. "Soon they be coming at night to see what else come down."

The police regularly searched the beach for bales of

marijuana or tightly bound packages of cocaine that might have been dropped from the planes. The islands were dotted with little airstrips — there were over 20 on Andros alone — and it wasn't uncommon to see the splayed hulks of small planes hanging in trees. At Norman's Cay, there was a complete DC-3 jammed in the sand and a couple of feet of water. That plane had come from the Guajira Peninsula, Burnett told me, in Colombia. I had seen a soggy bale wallowing in front of my terrace one morning.

There were many stories.

"Voodoo!" said Seymour Dufresne. "They take something that belongs to someone, bang it up and write on it, use it to make a curse. Don't mean nothing." He was a Haitian, but not a believer.

"A piece of garbage from the ocean," said Mrs. Holborne, at the Club. She had an opinion on everything. "Who cares?" She could not be interested in anything the villagers found so compelling.

"It's not far from your place, Tom," Burnett said, fiddling with his pipe. We were standing by the Club bar. "You ought to go see it, tell us what you think."

Tom Hargreaves said he thought he probably would do just that, as soon as he could find the time.

"Don't believe everything you hear," I said to Winnie, although I knew this was futile advice. "How do you know it's a satellite?"

"Mr. Hargreaves, he said so!" She was triumphant.

I heard it from Madame Dell who did my sheets. I heard it

from Mrs. Rainey when I went to buy fish. I heard it from Drover while he wrapped my frozen beef. I heard it from Seymour Dufresne in the harbour. I heard it from Vero at the Terrace Bar.

"There might be more stuff out there," Vero said. "Maybe some radio parts. Controls. We got to leave everything there, in case the police come. Besides, might be radioactive."

I asked Mary Hargreaves about it when she came into the bank.

"Oh, you know how people exaggerate," she said.

Three weeks after Vero's discovery, people were still heading to the beach for a look. At first guests from the hotel, for whom it was only a short walk, then visitors from the yachts in the harbour and tourists from Marsh Harbour and Treasure Cay. A photographer came from Great Abaco and Vero's picture was in the paper; they had it taped up behind the bar, just underneath the poem about Goombay Smash. Even the Yacht Club had developed an interest.

"You think they'll send someone out here to investigate?" Burnett asked Hargreaves. Hargreaves was relishing his celebrity.

"Oh, I wouldn't be too surprised," said Tom, "wouldn't be too surprised at all."

In fact when I told him several days later that a couple of U.S. military men had been in to see me, he was very surprised; he turned quite pale.

"You know where this old Soviet satellite is?" the tall one had said. He was the metals and aerospace expert, from the Defence Department. The other was CIA. They showed me their plastic-coated identification cards, their pictures on one side, the great eagle with the arrows in its claw on the other.

"Walk to the end of the Queen's Highway, then left. Follow the path that runs behind the graveyard."

"The graveyard? Jesus, where's that again?"

So I offered to take them.

You could tell where the satellite was by the number of tourists milling around. People were taking pictures. Some boys had a bonfire on the beach. One was selling beer from a Styrofoam cooler.

The thing itself was a curved piece of silvery-grey metal, perhaps five feet long, two feet wide at the base and tapered to a ragged point at the end. On the inside of the curved metal skin were what looked like tubular ribs, sheared bolts, several bits of bent, hanging metal. On the outside, about halfway down, there was a painted blue stripe and just below that, faded and peeling, a large blue letter, *P* or *R*.

The men from Washington sent the tourists away and began their examination. They were very thorough. They used magnifying glasses, micrometers and what looked to me like a Geiger counter. They also had something that enabled them to estimate density and God knows what else. I had to get back to the bank so I left them to their business.

They dropped in at my office on their way back, about an hour and a half later. It was very hot and the taller man kept wiping his face with a handkerchief. He said the metal was very light and could have easily been carried by the wind.

"Wonder how that rumour got started," he said.

"Did you talk to Hargreaves?" I asked.

"Who is Hargreaves?" he said.

"The guy who called you over here," I said. "Ex-Foreign Service."

"No one called us over," he said.

"Some story in the newspaper," he said. "We had to check." He produced a clipping, the same one taped to the wall behind Vero's bar. "You keep it," he said, "as a souvenir."

"Tom Hargreaves," he said, ruminating. "Name's familiar

from when I was in State. Economics Section, was it? No, I know! Trade and Consular Affairs, some industry officer or other, that's it. Wasn't he in London?"

We had a drink next door and then I accompanied them to the pier.

"So? What did they say?" said Mrs. Holborne. I hesitated for only a moment, but she caught it. "Just a piece of garbage!" She had a shrill voice. "I knew it!"

The Hargreaves stood behind Mrs. Holborne. Tom stared at the floor. Mary watched me. For once her hands were still. The Club had fallen silent. Even the steward was watching.

"They said it was the remains of a Russian satellite," I said. And then, getting carried away, I added, "They said it is no longer radioactive, that the core had burned itself out re-entering the atmosphere. The remote sensing equipment landed elsewhere and they have recovered most of it." I paused. "That is all I am permitted to say."

The party resumed.

A few days later Tom moved his business from Nassau over to me. It was substantial, more than either Burnett or I had expected.

And there was a dividend. The only paper the story had been in was the Marsh Harbour weekly. It hadn't been in any of the other Bahamian or Florida papers. I was gazing at the clipping, which I'd placed beneath the plastic cover on my desk blotter, when it struck me. I strolled across the Queen's Highway to the Terrace and took a seat at the bar. Vero's new motorcycle was leaning against the side of the thatched hut.

"Nice wheels," I said. "Where did you get it?"

He shrugged his shoulders.

"Those things cost, what, maybe U.S.$6,000? What do you earn here? Three bucks an hour for about 10 hours a week?"

That came to under $2,000 a year. Living was cheap in the islands, but not that cheap. I pulled the newspaper photo and said, "Maybe you would like this back, as a souvenir."

The masking tape on the blank space on the wall behind Vero matched the ripped masking tape on the clipping in my hand.

"It was you who contacted the men from Washington," I said. "You thought it was a Russian satellite all right, just like everyone else, and you wanted to make sure you got credit for finding it, only you knew Hargreaves wasn't CIA. You knew because *you* are the CIA contact on this island, Vero. Your job is to keep an eye on the Haitians, the Nicaraguans, especially the Cubans. That's why you have six grand to spend on a motorcycle."

"Hey, what you want, man?" said Vero.

"Nothing," I said. I took a sip of my rum. "So where do you do your banking?"

Pigeon Cay, November

Annie has taken to keeping some of her things at my place: her hairbrush, the white terry cloth robe I gave her, a bar of the scented soap she likes. I've cleared out several drawers and a cupboard for her. When I asked if she wanted more, she stared at me with fire in her eyes, suddenly angry.

Every day I see the schoolchildren passing by the open door of the bank. Karen and I never wanted children. I could only imagine the noise and tears, the temper tantrums. Karen wanted the life of a musician: fame and travel. And I remember afternoon parties at the homes of our bearded schoolteacher friends, amateur artists and folk-musicians, makers of stout tables and wooden toys: children of the 60s. Their own children ran wild in the kitchen, on back lawns, laughing, crying, innocent....

I cannot imagine Annie fitting in with those kinds of people. One of the things I like about her is that she is so different from my past life. I sometimes wonder if any children we might have could make a home off the island, whether she would really want to be a mother again, after 16 years and a daughter who will likely soon be a mother herself. I avoid her questions.

Meanwhile, Burnett has been proven right: not only are there U.S. agents here, the army has come and there have been a couple of rusty old freighters seen off Tilloo Cay, small, to navigate the inner passage.

Later

Half awake, roused by the squawking of the CB, I reached out, knocked over *The Ugly American* and *Burmese Days*, groping in the dark. I spilled rum on the floor, all over these pages. The ink is running. The lines are as blurry as my vision. The smell fills the room.

Tonight Azalea was picked up by the police outside one of the hotels across the channel. She had been drinking. She had been assaulted. She may have been raped.

Annie's left. I said I'd go with her, of course, but she said, no, everything was ruined now, she would get her mother to accompany her, as she knows Constable MacMahon. The three of them would cross the channel. She said she wasn't expecting me to come along; there were lots of others she could count on. She would call if she needed help.

I've had too much to drink. Maybe it has something to do with the bank, the tourists, Burnett and Healey, the Yacht Club, not giving Azalea the job in the first place and (what does Tommas say?) "the fucking United States." I've seen enough of the men she blames: at the bank, at the Club, smug and self-satisfied. I've seen enough of the tourists, too. I don't like the drugs any more than she does. But I'm not Healey. Why do I feel guilty?

Eight

Drover came in one morning with a problem: the freight boat had arrived three days early and he needed cash to pay for his order. There was no profit in it for the bank, but if I didn't give him the money Drover would go to Schindler at the Riverside. Schindler always had money.

"You wouldn't want that, would you, Mr. Rennison? You and me would be supporting the drug trade," said Drover.

"Why is the freight boat early?"

"Bringing soldiers over," he said.

After I'd given Drover the money, I shut the door, closed the safe and asked Winnie to begin the reconciliation. There was a knock at the door.

"Ignore it," I said to Winnie. "We're closed."

She looked past me, out the window.

"What is it?" I asked

A clatter on the sidewalk and then the door crashes in, splintering the frame and shattering the metal catch. Two soldiers burst into the room with a third behind. This last held the arm of an old man.

"You know him?" the soldier asked. He jerked the old man toward me, his body like a rag doll's. The man's collar was ripped, his hair matted. The officer pushed him onto my desk. Blood dripped onto the floor. Outside, a crowd started to gather.

"You know him?"

The plastic nametag on the soldier's chest said Lieutenant Bottrel. Bottrel was the commander of the local detachment of the Defence Force, rumoured to be a friend of Schindler's.

I could smell oil from the soldiers' guns, sweat from the clothing of the old man. The only sound was the whir of the ceiling fan.

The old man's name was Jimmy O'Brian. He owned the Casuarina, a small and decrepit restaurant up the creek where the water turned rank and brackish. The Casuarina had been patronized by boat builders, fishermen and sail makers, but business had declined. Jimmy had been to see me about a loan several months before. He'd taken me upstairs to the rooms above the café, which he had once rented to migrant forest workers and fishermen. The place smelled of rotting wood. Cobwebs shrouded the windows, but you could still see a view of the entire island and the outer channel. Through the tops of the palms, the Atlantic roiled and smoked against the reef. I looked down the harbour to the lighthouse, past the gap to Eagle Rock and the green sea. The south window faced upstream to the mangrove swamp and the far side of the island, hazy in the distance.

There were a couple of chairs, an ashtray, some empty bottles nearby. Jimmy handed me a pair of binoculars. He planned to open a bar for tourists visiting the islands on yachts.

When I told Healey I'd approved the loan, he rolled his eyes. "Jimmy says he can raise about $20,000 on his own," I said.

"Somebody must think he knows what he's doing."

"No," I said to the officer, pressing Jimmy against my desk. "I don't know him."

"You didn't give him money?"

"No." Only a slight lie. Jimmy had not used the loan because of a string of bad luck. Someone left the shutters open and rain lashed into the upstairs rooms, ruining the walls; a crawfish boat rammed into one of the piers, knocking it from under the supporting beam.

Jimmy twisted his head, struggling on the desktop. One of the soldiers brought the butt of his rifle down on Jimmy's back and he sprawled on the floor. They dragged him away.

Soon after they left I called on Tom Hargreaves — we were supposed to join some others for tennis down at Burnett's plantation — but he had not yet returned from his weekly trip across the channel.

I waited on the side terrace, to avoid the steady wind from the Atlantic. The growth was dense: red hibiscus, pale oleander and bougainvillaea spilled from the garden into the forest beyond the wall. Sunlight filtered through the palms and frangipani to the spiky ferns and purple oyster plants. When the wind blew, the light shifted from green to yellow, as though underwater, and warm air hissed through the sea grapes, shuffling the leaves.

A dark face appeared before me. I jumped. Just the Hargreaves' maid.

Then, as far along the rise as I could see, I noticed soldiers struggling through the underbrush, khaki and olive among the flashing leaves. They used their guns as shields against the snapping branches and had started their search on the beach below the low cliffs before making their way through the scrub, up the ridge, across the isthmus to Black Creek. A small plane approached from the sea, swooped low over the harbour.

Moments later Mary Hargreaves came onto the terrace. "Tom called," she said. She was even jumpier than usual. "He's going straight to Burnett's place. Meet him there. Walk along the beach, rather than up the road, if you want to avoid the soldiers."

"They were looking for drugs," said Tom Hargreaves. "Part of some kind of task force."

"There must have been a tip-off," said Burnett. We were sitting on his deck facing the ocean, drinking rum and fruit juice. I told them about Lieutenant Bottrel's visit to the bank.

"I wonder what Bottrel had to do with the operation," said Hargreaves. "These fellows sweeping the island are not his regular flunkies, they're the *real* army, from the capital."

Burnett fiddled with his pipe. He said, facing me, "I recommend you lie low. Don't say anything. You might close early for the next day or two. Don't take any big deposits. We don't want an investigation, like over on Bimini." There, a man had strolled into the bank and deposited $750,000 in cash. There had been congressional investigations and subpoenas.

In the sky, an airplane swooped and dipped, criss-crossing the island.

"Another drink?" said Hargreaves.

The searchers found a couple of speedboats in the swamp. Travelling flat out at 90 miles an hour between the islands and Miami, they would have been used perhaps three or four times until the engines burned out or the propeller shafts cracked, then abandoned.

Jimmy spent three nights in the cell beneath the post office. Saturday night Bottrel and the two soldiers drank and caroused in the billiard room of the Riverside. I heard their shouting, the pounding of the jukebox, from my house at the far end of the harbour. In the morning Schindler paid the soldiers' bill.

On Monday, they marched Jimmy to their boat at the government pier. I saw him later at the window of the listing second floor of the Casuarina.

A few days later a stranger walked into the bank: faded polo shirt, worn canvas shorts, leather Top Siders, sunglasses on straps. Wall Street was my guess, a yachtsman with an educated Yankee accent. But it turned out to be Midwestern.

"Buy you a drink?" he said. He glanced at Winnie to indicate he wanted to speak to me alone. I rose from my desk. We crossed the road to the Majestic. He showed me his identification and my heart sank. I hoped Healey wouldn't see us, or, even worse, Burnett. I declined the offer of lunch.

"It's okay," he said. "You're the only guy who knows I'm here. Supposed to be undercover. Got a Nonesuch in the harbour."

He was with the United States Drug Enforcement Agency. There was a sea breeze coming in from Portugal, but I felt myself starting to sweat.

"You know why I'm here," he said.

"I don't see how I can help you," I said.

"You run the only bank on the island," he said.

"There are banks at Swamp Harbour, some of the other islands," I said.

"We're watching them very carefully."

"What do you want?" I said.

"A sharp eye. You know who has money, who doesn't. Where deals happen. You have a house at the mouth of the harbour. Maybe you see things."

"You must have someone here," I said, "someone who can tell you what's going on."

He shrugged his shoulders. "Nobody we can count on. Besides, even if we think we know what's going on, we have no authority. We can pass on information, but you know the government here."

"I must be going," I said. "Our busiest time." I pushed my chair back from the table.

"Of course, I understand. I'll come with you."

I sat down again.

"What we need," he said, "is information to help us nab them in the States. You might take note of large cash deposits and withdrawals, transfers and drafts, doubtful business investments, authorizations for loans through other branches, names and dates. That sort of thing."

"There are laws about this sort of thing. Strict confidentiality. Even if I wanted to help you, I couldn't."

"I know all about the laws. But we have no such impediments in Florida. We can go after your branches in Broward and Dade, where we think people like, say, Schindler, make irregular transfers from Pigeon Cay. We can make sure your name is in the papers, yes?"

"But there's nothing I can tell you. I really must be going."

"Of course. Sorry to have kept you. If you change your mind, call me."

He gave me a card with the number and address of a marina in Pompano Beach, where I was to leave a message for a Mr. Lyon. I put the card in the bottom drawer of my desk.

I was roused by knocking at the door on a Sunday morning several weeks later. I'd slept poorly, kept awake by the halyard snapping against the flagpole in the wind.

"Mr. Rennison, you got to come. Bring your boat. Meet us at the pier," Drover said.

Outside it was still dark, a pearly grey. I winched the Zodiac down the concrete bank and dragged it across the sand to the water. I smelled burning wood from the refugee settlements. Figures like ghosts drifted at the end of the pier of the Majestic Hotel.

"What is it?" I asked.

"Man in the river," said Constable MacMahon when we got there. He poured a cup of coffee. "You take Seymour here and go on ahead, ask his mother what happened."

Up Black Creek, beyond the rotting wharves of the old schooner captains, were the back piers of the expatriates whose lavish houses stood beyond the ridge, facing the Atlantic. The passage narrowed. In the east the sky became pink, shot through with pale yellow.

Looming before us, the last building before the creek dissipated into a maze of streams and dark swamp impassable to all but the smallest boats, was the Casuarina Café. The main structure was leaning in the high winter tide, the corner of the front dining room under the surface, water lapping against the floorboards. The back of the building, a single storey built along the bank of the creek, was level and still open. Celia Dufresne, Seymour's mother, stood on the planks of the pier. She worked at the café and on weekends she slept in a lean-to at the rear of the building.

"He come out here to check on his boat," she said in a flat voice.

She gazed up the creek toward the mangrove swamp. The tide rose in greasy eddies.

We found Jimmy's boat around a bend in the river, not 50 yards from the café, wallowing to the gunwales, flayed lines trailing. Seymour hopped on the deck, stuck his head in the cabin window.

"Find anything?" I asked.

"Radio smashed," he said.

"Must have broken loose in the wind."

We spent three hours in the swamp; we travelled so far in that we could no longer use the motors, but had to paddle and pole among tangled roots and branches, working against the suction of the ebb tide.

We were told by Constable MacMahon that Jimmy O'Brian had had a heart attack while securing his lines in the wind the night before, fallen overboard and drowned, his body carried away by the tide.

Crossing the harbour, I noticed a boat that had not been anchored there before — markings crudely painted over, bristling with aerials, guns shrouded in thick black canvas — one of the U.S. Coast Guard vessels. The following morning the boat was gone, slipped away under cover of darkness.

"Look at this," Healey said. Spread out on the desk before him were graphs prepared by the Nassau office. He pointed, following the lines with two fingers of one hand. "A trend. Business down in your office, up everywhere else. What do you make of that? Here's something else. This line shows what happens to business this time of year. We get a slight falloff after Christmas, then more or less level until mid-March, then steadily falling business until the summer. Now here's Pigeon Cay. Business already below March levels."

"It's a mystery to me," I said.

"Well, you might check it out. Before Burnett does."

I called in at the Riverside Tavern and heard the crackle of the barman's radiophone. If anyone knew what was going on it would be Schindler. The day was so still I could almost hear him from his cruiser, 150 yards out in the harbour.

"Says he'll meet you, but not here," said the barman. "The hotel. Six o'clock."

From my table by the pool, I watched Schindler striding up the hill. He paused, removed his straw hat and wiped his forehead with a handkerchief. He was balding, his face was fleshy, with a broad nose and a squint.

"What about this old man, the fellow who was in trouble with the police?" said Schindler. He paused. "The restaurant owner who had all those…unfortunate accidents."

"O'Brian? He's dead."

Schindler signalled the bar for another drink. He said, "Did they find the body?"

"You think he's still alive?" I said.

"One hears rumours," said Schindler.

"Why don't you ask your friend Lieutenant Bottrel to look into it?"

"Mr. Rennison, you pay me a compliment, to imagine that a simple tavern owner such as myself would have any influence with the military."

"One hears rumours," I said.

Schindler smiled. "As a matter of fact — and only since you raise it — my impression is that Lieutenant Bottrel is routinely ignored by the government, that he is kept in the dark about operations in these islands, about our government's various co-operative ventures with the Americans."

"Perhaps that's because of his friendship with you," I said.

"I cannot believe that our 'friendship,' as you put it, is so widely known as that, Mr. Rennison. No. My impression is that Lieutenant Bottrel is incompetent. I believe you've had some dealings with him?"

"He's very competent with a rifle butt," I said.

"It is because of his fierce reputation that no one will speak. Whereas a man like yourself, Mr. Rennison, a banker, the only banker on the island, you have links throughout the community. I feel certain people would talk to you. The Haitians, for instance."

"What are you suggesting?"

"I'm not suggesting anything at all. I am commiserating. This is a small community. We are on the fringes here. We don't need trouble."

"What do you think the trouble is?"

"I think those soldiers frightened away the customers. These sweeps of the islands, the American boats in the channels, the joint task force, that's what hurting business."

"You mean the tavern business," I said.

"The tavern business, of course. And the banking business. As you have said, the trouble affects us all. Would you care for another drink?"

For a long time, Seymour Dufresne and a group of Haitian refugees had wanted a loan to mount some kind of salvage operation. It had always seemed doubtful. Now Burnett said to me, "I suppose you had better go and at least have a look."

I took a boat from the hotel and rowed across the harbour to the end of Horseshoe Bay. There was an opening cut through the mangroves to the stony shore. There, a path led through the bush. In the muddy lagoon and the small creek along the path were half-submerged, rotting boats.

I came to the first of the shanties. Haitians lived here, as well as refugees from Cuba and Central America. I crossed a stream of sewage, smelling the acrid smoke of burning silverwood. I asked one of the children who had started following me to take me to Seymour Dufresne.

The meeting lasted about half an hour. After I discussed the loan, I asked Seymour what he really knew about Jimmy O'Brian.

"Follow me," he said.

He led me through the scattered hulls among the trees until we came to Jimmy's boat. There were five three-quarter-inch holes bored neatly below the stain of the water line. I felt them with my fingers. They were recent.

"Where's Jimmy?" I asked.

Seymour shrugged his shoulders. "Gone." I asked him to take me to see his mother at the Casuarina.

Celia Dufresne sat outside with a couple of other old women, splicing ropes from the wrecks in the harbour. She nodded in response to my greeting. I offered her a cigarette and we sat in silence for a while: Seymour, the three old women and myself. At length, the other two women, with much effort, rose to their feet and left.

"I've seen Jimmy's boat. Five holes drilled in the hull."

I made a circle with my thumb and finger to suggest the size of the holes. Celia said nothing. I continued, "You said that morning that Jimmy went to check on his boat, that he never came back. What happened? How did he fall into the river?"

She glanced at her son. He gave her a look of warning, but she spoke anyway.

"He never fell over. He jumped, headed up the swamp with the tide before they come to get 'im."

"No heart attack?" I said. "No going out to look at the boat in the storm?"

"We were sitting in the kitchen after closing, before the wind come up. We heard noises. So Jimmy go outside. I guess he seen those holes in the boat, the water coming in, the radio and all like that. He turn around real fast, like he seen someone on the road. Then he jumps in the river, swimming across there, up the swamp. In the morning, when Constable MacMahon come around for his early coffee, like he do every morning, I tell him about Jimmy falling in."

She bent down, returning to her splicing. When I pushed my chair back against the wall, I noticed an aerial, newly attached.

"You got a new radio here?" I asked.

"A present," said Celia. "He gone to that place they got the dogs, the bar at Great Abaco. He wants to make a deal, come back to the café."

"When is he meeting them?" I asked.

"Midnight," said Celia.

Seymour stepped between us.

There was no answer when I knocked on the door of Tom Hargreaves' house. I opened the door and walked in, calling as I went. In the white room at the front of the house, on the ocean side, a gun lay on a table. Sunlight through the jalousie illuminated its oiled sheen like a flat colourless photograph.

"David! Let yourself in, did you? Caught me by surprise. Just cleaning things up a bit." In his hand Tom Hargreaves held an oily rag. He scooped up the gun.

"Browning automatic," he said. "Bought it in Miami after some drug-runners tried to board my cruiser, near More's Island. Has a nickel handle, almost a collector's item." He put the gun in a drawer.

"Care for a drink?"

"It's about Jimmy O'Brian."

"Oh?"

"The day the soldiers swept the island looking for drugs, you told us all about it. I was wondering how you knew, Tom, that's all. You were out all morning — I know because I waited for you here — and then you went straight to Burnett's place. You couldn't have heard anything on your radio. At least not that day."

Tom went pale.

"You know," he said.

"I know Jimmy O'Brian had a radio on that boat of his. I know he had found some money to put into the restaurant. I think he gave some money to Seymour Dufresne and the Haitians for the salvage operation."

"Twenty-five thousand dollars. Half by bank deposit at the start, the rest in cash when the operation was over. That's what Jimmy was getting from the Americans, drug enforcement people, in return for information. Where the boats came in, the drop-offs, things like that. There was a code, so I don't know exactly what he told them and I don't know how he knew what he did. But I heard them talking. They told him there was going to be a sweep, that's the day the first of Jimmy's money would go to a bank in Miami."

"That was also the day that Lieutenant Bottrel was here," I said. "He must have known too. What else?"

"What do you mean?"

"These Coast Guard boats in the channel, the task force; I think Jimmy is still at it. I was in the Haitian village. There's a new high frequency radio there."

"Ah, so that's where he is," said Hargreaves. "But the last message was sent over 10 days ago now. He must be afraid."

"He should be. I think somebody almost got to him the night of the storm. Would anyone else know about this?"

"No one else in the islands has a radio like mine," said Hargreaves. He glanced at the drawer.

As soon as I heard that the meeting with Jimmy O'Brian had been moved forward, I ran from the bank down the Queen's Highway to Constable MacMahon's house. I told him to get hold of the task force in any way he could, to tell someone to get to the bar on Great Abaco as soon as possible. I left by the back door and scrambled down the embankment, through the frangipani to the government pier. The sun was sinking below the height of land behind the lighthouse. I waved, then shouted to Ti-Paul, who was sitting at the taxi wharf on the far side of the harbour.

Night fell as we crossed the channel. We landed at a solitary pier jutting out from trees along the dark shore. Ti-Paul had called a taxi van on his radiophone; it was waiting at the pier, by a road that led up the hill and into the forest. I sat on an iron bench in the back of the van, hanging on as we rattled over pot-holed roads.

"What you goin' there for, mister?" the driver asked me. "No fights tonight."

"You bring anyone else out here today?" I asked.

"No, but I seen some guy walking along this road late afternoon."

Forty minutes later he let me out at the side of the bar, a ramshackle place, one of three buildings in a clearing in the bush. Now the moon made the night bright. The parking lot was empty except for a battered jeep. Inside the bar there was a slow-moving fan, the smell of smoke and mildew. Dim yellow bulbs lit bottles behind the bar. The place was almost empty.

"He was here. Maybe half an hour ago."

"Anyone else?"

"Three soldiers. Defence Force guys. I think they all gone out back to look at the dogs."

I walked along the cinder path, which wound through the trees, heard the sound of barking and snarling. I came to a clearing at the edge of a pool of light. The sloping sides of the pit — about 15 feet deep and 25 feet across — were lit by a light on a pole to my right. Beneath the pole were the cages and in front of these stood four men. Bottrel stood feet slightly apart, watching. He held a stubby shotgun in his hand. The other two men held Jimmy O'Brian, one on each arm. They were standing in front of a cage with two snarling dogs. All of them were looking at me.

"We be interrogating someone," said Bottrel. "You better be getting along."

Jimmy pulled free and leapt onto Bottrel's back. The dogs

were in a frenzy. Bottrel turned and fired one shot. The bullet struck Jimmy with a force that threw him off his feet.

In slow motion Bottrel turned, bringing the gun in his extended arm to chest level. The muzzle pointed at me. How many shells did a shotgun hold? Was it two, or did the newer ones have clips? I saw his finger on the trigger. I lurched forward into the darkness of the pit. The shot echoed in my ears. As I tumbled, I hit my head. People swarmed out of the bush and down the earthen sides of the pit. I hit the ground, dazed. There was a roaring sound and then I was blinded by spotlights shining from a hovering helicopter.

Some weeks later the lawyers came from Freeport to see about Jimmy O'Brian's will and possessions. I took them to the empty restaurant. There was a buyer for the Casuarina, they told me, willing to pay an excellent price. He was going to tear the place down. Upstairs, Jimmy's binoculars were still on the table.

Pigeon Cay, February

A surprise to all of us about Tom and Mary Hargreaves. What can Tom have been thinking? The woman was young enough to be his daughter. Is it something about this place, these long warm nights? I'm getting the story down, perhaps with one or two additional details, borrowing a bit from a murder on Eluthera I read about in the papers. Increasingly the stories are about small-time corruption, squalid infidelities, yearnings, hopes, the dreams people have that somewhere, some time in the future, they will glimpse perfection.

Annie has returned, but she is distant, hasn't forgiven me. As soon as I heard she was back on the island I sent her a note, tried to call her on the radio, even took a taxi to the other end of the island and dropped in at the Goombay Bar. It was morning and the place smelled of disinfectant. I saw her briefly, but she said she was working, was too busy to talk. A couple of days later, she called me on the CB radio from the bar. The conversation was stilted. I asked her about Azalea. She said a couple of American tourists did it, they think, only 25 years old, from New York. Nothing will happen to them now.

Gregor Robinson

Annie wants to get her out of here, go to the U.S., Canada.

Now we were on shaky ground. Was this why she had called me? Annie was an illegal immigrant to Pigeon Cay, though she's been here years now. The only way she can move again is as an illegal immigrant. She can buy fake papers. Or she could get married.

Swan, the owner of the Hotel Paradiso, has asked for an increase in his revolving line of credit. Bit of a mystery what he needs it for; the place is run-down, near miasmic Fish Mangrove. I can't believe they do much business. He wouldn't show me the books, but Healey says it doesn't matter; we've dealt with him before and he's good for the money. He used to be in shipping. Perhaps he is one of the new entrepreneurs who operate refugee scams, take people's life savings in return for the promise of delivering them to the U.S., and then disappear with the down payments. All sorts of human flotsam and jetsam wash up here, like those four on the boat....

Yesterday I added a new specimen to the list of local flora. *Bunchosia glandulosa*, the botanical name for the rather rare tree known as pain-in-back. Wonderful name. Grows up to 20 feet high, with a slender trunk and rough bark. The leaves are green and shiny, shaped like weeping willow leaves and the fruit is a round, smooth berry, orangy-red in colour and about a third of an inch across. I can find no one to tell me whether it causes pain or cures pain.

Nine

As it happened, I was the first to set eyes on them. I looked out the window one morning, through the lemon-light of the frangipani leaves, and saw them drop anchor. I heard the splash, the unreeling chain. The yachts from the Carolinas and New England would not be back until fall and the basin was almost empty.

The boat was an old motor-sailer and had a high cabin house with grey woodwork. The sail wrapped round the boom in mottled lumps. Three people descended the ladder single file into a dinghy: two men and a woman in their early 20s. The woman and one of the men were blond. The third was dark and thin, more a boy than a man, yet he was the leader; he hurried the others along. They set off, rowing quickly, apparently eager to be ashore.

When they reached the pier, the dark-haired man spoke to one of the Haitians waiting for the noon ferry to come in. Rolled cigarettes changed hands and some arrangement was made. They hoisted their packs and strolled down the road between the casuarinas and the tall palms, away from the village. Ti-Paul towed their dinghy back to the motor-sailer. He called up to a fourth who had come up from below decks: a tall, white-blond man.

Gregor Robinson

At 12:30 that day, Ti-Paul came in with cash receipts from the ferry. The three young people had hitched a cruise with a white-blond stranger from Green Turtle Cay, half a day's sail across the Sea of Abaco.

"I think they're here for a while," he said. "The girl's been seasick, even just coming from Turtle Cay. She said she's not going on any boat again — not for a long time."

By sunset I knew that they had set up camp down the beach on the Atlantic side, past Annie's place, at the end of the reef. Tom Hargreaves had been out in his jeep and saw them turn off the road and take the trail between the dunes.

The blond girl was Harriet Jones. She was from Elmira, New York. She had come into the bank to cash a traveller's cheque.

"You cashing only a hundred bucks?" said the dark-haired boy one of them called Axel. There was the smell of marijuana about them.

"It's all I have left," she said. Axel watched intently as Winnie counted out the bills.

"Any place we can go fishing?" Axel asked. "Dive for conch, maybe catch some lobster?"

I told them that lobster fishing was strictly regulated and that conch was in deeper waters this time of year. They ought to talk to Mrs. Rainey. Her husband sometimes took visitors out to sea for a small fee.

The only other time I saw them was from Tom Hargreaves' deck. I'd dropped over with some papers for him to sign and he asked me in for a drink. There was a pair of binoculars on the table next to where we sat facing the Atlantic. The visitors were camped in front of the graveyard just the south of Hargreaves'

house. They had built a lean-to of driftwood, silverwood branches and palm leaves. He had made a study of their habits.

"That's only for their food and pack, a little shelter if it rains," said Hargreaves. "They live and sleep in the open, under the sky."

One day he'd gone to ask that they be careful of sparks that might be carried by the wind to the dry grasses behind the beach. He showed them how to make a banked fire, something he'd learned 35 years before, in his own youth, at summer camp in Maine.

When Mary went in to see about the dinner, he handed me the binoculars. "Take a look if you like," he said.

But I could see them even without the binoculars. It was a warm night. They were body surfing. They were nude.

"Can't they see us?" I asked. Tom was wearing a large straw hat to protect his scaly forehead from the sun. It was a hat he often wore; it would be visible from much farther down the beach than their campfire.

"Sun's behind us now, we're in the shadows," he said.

Harriet Jones strode from the water. She ran her hands along the sides of her head, squeezing the seawater from her hair. She was looking toward the sunset and I think she might have noticed us watching as she entered the lean-to. The boys wrapped towels around themselves and began the business of setting the fire.

There was a bustling behind us, the clink of ice, Tom Hargreaves coughing. Mary had returned. Tom harrumphed, began to talk. He said he thought the campers were ruining the place, ought to get the police after them. Mary said nothing.

I expected the man on the boat to drop in at the bank too. Most visitors do, if not for money then at least to make themselves known; the bank served as a kind of unofficial consulate. He didn't come in, but because of my vantage point overlooking the harbour I saw more of him than anybody else. I saw him working on his boat, rowing ashore to buy supplies, walking along the road with his loping stride, or strolling along the edge of the surf.

He had been looking for the girl.

A few mornings later, I threw open the shutters and saw that his boat was gone; the next morning it was back again. Sometimes he was gone and back the same day. And even though he lived on the boat, he'd taken a room at the Majestic, one of the cheap ones at the back.

It came up a few hours later at lunch with the Hargreaves and Madame Grumbacher.

"Does he use it much?" Tom asked Madame Grumbacher.

"You know better than to ask me that," she said. She'd been in the islands for 20 years, yet she still spoke with a German accent.

Mary sat across the table from us, waiting. She thought Tom drank too much. She dabbed at her forehead with a pink handkerchief.

Six weeks later the blond stranger from the boat lay dead in a back room at the Majestic. Constable MacMahon stood behind me in his large regulation shoes, asking whether I knew of anyone who owned a .32.

Tom Hargreaves owned a .32; bought it secondhand in Miami, after the trouble at More's Island. It was a small Browning automatic with a nickel handle, a classic. I'd caught him polishing the thing a while back and the smell of oil had filled the house, forcing Mary Hargreaves, who hated the sea breeze, to throw open the windows.

I didn't mention this to Constable MacMahon.

The corpse was wearing baggy white pants, no shirt, no shoes. He would have been about 40. He had fine features. Despite the unkempt hair, the shadow of his unshaven face and the weathered skin, he was good looking; you could see that even in death.

The room was filled with the smell of cooking oil from the kitchen vents below the window.

"Is that the fellow from the boat?" asked Constable MacMahon.

"It's him," I said.

He'd been shot no more than five hours before, according to Dr. Cutter, around noon, when the village was at its busiest and the freight boat was unloading and the big fans in the hotel kitchens were spinning full blast. No one heard a thing. His name was Ainsley; MacMahon found it by going through his wallet. Five hundred U.S. was found in the top drawer of the dresser. The cash, the boat that was in and out of the harbour, this room, which might serve as a business venue for nervous customers, added up.

"Right," said Constable MacMahon. "Now I search the boat."

For me, there was the matter of the gun.

Mary Hargreaves did not like unannounced visits. Even though I had my briefcase and the pretext of business, she was reluctant to ask me in. The house had been ransacked. Two of the front windows were smashed, furniture overturned, books pulled from the shelves, food from the pantry and refrigerator strewn across the floors and carpets. The house smelled of liquor, bottles smashed against the walls.

Tom had been fishing; Mary had left early to do the shopping across the channel. They had returned to find this.

"Who do you think it was?" I asked.

I thought Mary was about to answer when Hargreaves came from behind and interrupted. "No idea," he said.

"Did they take anything?"

"Not that I can see." He was brusque. There was something he wasn't telling me. When Mary left the room, I asked again, "Is anything missing?"

He stared, but said nothing. I told him that the man from the boat was dead in his room in the Majestic Hotel. Shot with a .32-calibre bullet.

"You must tell the police about this," I said, sweeping my hand across the debris.

"Why?" said Hargreaves.

"Because otherwise they will think you killed him."

"Constable MacMahon doesn't know that I have a .32-calibre pistol. Unless you told him. So no one will think anything."

Hargreaves walked me up the path: he wanted a word in private, away from Mary.

"The girl, you know, on the beach, she cashed some sort of traveller's cheque?" I was surprised he knew this. I nodded. He took off his hat, scratched his forehead. "You know her name then, where she's from and so on?" I nodded again.

"David, you and I are friends. I would appreciate it if you didn't mention any of these details — about the girl, I mean — to Constable MacMahon, should he ask."

"Speak of the devil," I said. Constable MacMahon came

clopping along the sidewalk. Hargreaves' grip on my elbow tightened.

Constable MacMahon had not come to see him. He was on his way to the beach, to the campsite. I walked with him.

He brought me up to speed. The man from the boat was indeed a dealer, small-time.

"I found a few packets of the stuff on the boat, all neatly done up the way they do for the tourists," Constable MacMahon said.

However, the theory of the room at the Majestic as a place for drug transactions was falling apart. No one had visited the man there (Madame Grumbacher confirmed this) and there were no drugs in the room.

We reached the end of the Queen's Highway and turned toward the beach and the sound of the surf. As we walked through the old cemetery, I noticed a figure on Hargreaves' deck.

The trio must have left in a hurry; the fire pit was still warm. While MacMahon sifted through the ashes, I strolled up the bank behind the campsite. Beneath the brambles and sea grapes I spotted Hargreaves' binoculars, encrusted with white salt.

"Find anything?" said Constable MacMahon.

"No," I answered.

Constable MacMahon discovered that Hargreaves owned a .32 without my help and he learned about the break-in, too. The gun was never found; not surprising, with the Atlantic and the Sea of Abaco in which to dispose of it. As for the visitors, the same day the body was found Ti-Paul ferried them across the channel to the plane to Fort Lauderdale. Their money problems had apparently been resolved.

"They stole the gun from Hargreaves," said Constable MacMahon. We were sitting at the bar of the Majestic. "I don't think they had in mind to use it at first. They were up there to teach Mr. Hargreaves a little lesson."

It was something everyone in the village knew by now: Hargreaves had been watching the girl with his binoculars. He kept watching her even after the two men warned him, Constable MacMahon said, until finally they came and ransacked the place. They took the binoculars and the gun.

"How do you know all this?" I asked.

"Can't tell you that. We must protect our sources." He took a noisy gulp of beer and continued. "As for the murder, the same old story. Axel must have seen Harriet and the guy from the boat together on the beach. The Haitians confirmed that she had been seen with an older fellow. Axel had Mr. Hargreaves' gun, so he killed his competition. Axel and Harriet were having it off as well."

"The girl was prone to seasickness," MacMahon told us. "She had vowed to stay off boats. That's why the guy took the room."

"Have another beer, Constable," I said.

"Thank you, sir, I believe I will," said Constable MacMahon. "As for poor Mr. Hargreaves, Mary is leaving him."

A few days later, Mary Hargreaves came into the bank. She wanted to look after some loose ends, she said; she was leaving the island for good. There would no longer be a joint account.

Mary went carefully over the records. Something caught her eye, a couple of recent transactions, rather large cheques made out to cash.

"Ah, you see!" she said. "He even gave her money, the bastard!"

Mary had made her own decision to tip off MacMahon about the gun. Hargreaves must have thought until the end that she hadn't known. But wives always know. Axel had shot the wrong man.

Pigeon Cay, May

Even here, shot through with tropical light, the forest is mysterious. Impossible, at least for me, to know even a fraction of the species. Certain local plants are used for medical and religious purposes. Some cause hallucinations, others, a coma-like trance. Despite what the ethnologists and anthropologists say, knowledge among the local people of the powers of these plants is growing. I think it has to do with the coming of the Haitians, the Cubans (there is even a form of Santería here), a new interest in indigenous customs.

Ritual and ceremonial use of plants go hand in hand with superstitions and rumours of ghosts. In Pigeon Cay, you're not supposed to walk between the cholera cemetery and the ocean at night; you must remain always on the road, on the sea side of the fence. There's an abandoned villa on an island off North Point that once belonged to a rum smuggler who was supposed to have been murdered and fed to the sharks, so that island, too, is haunted. And in the forests, in the Haitian settlements: voodoo. Madame Grumbacher had a Haitian servant, Toussignant, who is said to be a zombie.

Gregor Robinson

It can get to you. I heard a barking dog one night when I slept on the sailboat outside the mouth of the harbour. I thought someone had come aboard. "It was the ghost dog of the mangrove swamp," Burnett said. He, of all people, seems to believe.

A few nights ago, walking home from the Goombay Bar on a stormy night, I passed by a house under construction. In a flash of lightning I thought I saw a skull flicker against the scaffolding, implanted in the stone foundation.

Annie has taken me back. Her mother is being bundled off to another island nearby, to live with Annie's aunt. She has transferred her business to another bank, including a loan, and Healey thinks she is planning to leave. I cannot think too far ahead.

In the darkness she is more passionate than ever. I wonder if we will last or if, like many whom happiness has eluded, I am powerfully drawn to ruin. I find comfort in imperfections, like the mottled birthmark on Annie's lower back.

Ten

It was past midnight and Burnett and I had finished our business, but Irish whisky and a steady rain, both rare in the islands, kept us late. Mrs. Hamish had cleared the dinner dishes and gone to bed. Now the whisky bottle stood almost empty on the table between us and we sat silently, listening to the gurgle of the water running down the roof and into the concrete cistern beneath the floor. The rain seemed to be letting up. It was difficult to tell with that sibilant rush, the drumming on the windowpanes drowning out the sound of the surf below.

I was planning to walk home along the path that wound through the scrub growth above the beach; it was the shortest route from Burnett's house to the village. I waited for the rain to stop.

"Not so much the rain as the night you have to be careful of," said Burnett. "Voodoo," he added, with exaggeration. "Feeding the *loa*."

I told him I wasn't afraid of the dark. I wasn't superstitious.

"All the same, easy to get lost." He gestured toward the blackened windowpane. "The paths criss-cross and twist back on one another. Before you know it, you wind up in the bush at the other end of the island. Completely lost. Zombie country." He grinned. "Tell you what: when the rain lets up, I'll get Tommas to drive you home."

Tommas lived in a hut on a corner of Burnett's property and still did the odd job around the plantation despite his dedication to writing. He, too, had to eat. He would resent being roused in the middle of the night to drive me home. But there was little choice, for Burnett had begun the laborious business of cleaning his pipe; soon he was filling it with fresh tobacco.

"I ever tell you about Taffy?" he said, lifting his eyes from the task.

With a day's growth, his iron hair slicked back, his foul pipe and the bright gleam of his blue eyes, Burnett looked like an old sailor. He liked to talk. Living alone in the islands had made him garrulous and a terrible gossip. I poured myself another whisky, the one I'd declined a moment before.

"Taffy, that's what everyone called him," Burnett said. "He was an Englishman. Actually, I'd met him in London several years earlier, through my squash club. He still had the damn tie, used to wear it to the Yacht Club on Saturday nights. In England he'd been some kind of businessman, direct sales and patent medicines, that kind of thing; you didn't want to go into it too closely. He'd retired from all that and gone back to his first love, schoolteaching. He came out to see about starting a school here. He was here maybe six or seven months altogether, but it never came to anything. Point is, he was like you, undaunted by the prospect of walking in the woods. 'Whatever happens, you come to the sea,' he used to say, 'all you do is follow the coast. One way or another, you come to a pier, somebody's house. Then you're home free.' "

"Something in that," I said.

"Said he didn't believe in voodoo either, of course. Made a great point of saying it was mumbo-jumbo, the going into trances and so forth, a religion for the ignorant. After all, he was English. 'The Brits are not hysterical,' he said. 'Sensible people. You saw it in the Blitz, old boy.' "

"Did he actually call you 'old boy'?"

"All the time," said Burnett. "Hexing, spells, the pointing of the bone, whatever you call it, he didn't believe in any of it."

"Do you?"

"No, or rather, I don't like to say," said Burnett. "It's like the Holy Ghost, the Trinity. What's all that? You tell me. But here it's in the air. My housekeeper is a sensible woman, but talk to her on Christmas Eve or New Year's and she won't leave the village. You can hear the drums from the centre of the island wherever you go. If you interrupt the ceremony, the *hougan* will throw a curse."

He looked at me, pausing for effect. Outside the shutters rattled as the wind rose. Burnett said, "Have you ever seen a zombie?"

"Only on 'The Late Show'," I said.

"You know that fellow Toussignant, who sweeps the sidewalk in front of the hotel, cleans up the garbage bins? Toussignant used to work on a forest plantation on Great Abaco. After the place closed he wandered around in the scrub behind Marsh Harbour. People gave him food. Then one of the refugees saw him, fellow from the north, near Cap Haitian. He said he knew Toussignant, that he'd died several years before. No one there would have much to do with him after that; that's when Madame Grumbacher brought him over here."

"What do *you* think?" I asked.

"It's not what I think," said Burnett. "It's what happens. The *hougan* throws a curse, the victim gets sick and dies."

"Do people actually get sick and die?" I asked.

"Of course people get sick and die. All the time. Always will.

Gregor Robinson

Nothing to do with voodoo. Plain illness or maybe poison, that's what Taffy used to say. He'd researched it. When Taffy first came here he used to travel a lot, almost every week. He said it was to talk to people about the school, financial people and so on, government officials. But it was always to places like Grand Cayman, Free Town, places where they have the casinos. Easy money.

"This school of his should have given us a clue: he kept changing the notion of what the thing was for. First it was supposed to be art and drama — he even joined the Strawboaters, who perform in the Methodist Chapel, and he did a very nice Boris Karloff in *Arsenic and Old Lace*. Then he started talking about the project as some kind of science school, a centre for nature studies, like that place over on Andros. Learn all about plants, he said. Finally it was anthropology, which was logical because Taffy was something of an anthropologist himself. There would be field trips to remote places, examine the connections with Africa and so on.

"It turned out he'd visited every casino in the West Indies. Then he started gambling here. There's a game at the Majestic Hotel on Saturday nights when the dart league plays. He got into that, but it wasn't enough. He asked around at the poolroom at the Riverside, at the marina, down at the government pier. Word got out. One day Ti-Paul approached, asked Taffy if he wanted to play down at the place where Annie works."

The Goombay Bar was at the far end of the island, at the mouth of Fish Mangrove. If the wind was low you could sometimes hear the throaty roar of speedboats leaving the lagoon in the middle of the night.

"There's often a big game there," Burnett said. "People from Miami, the other islands. The first few nights Taffy did well, seemed to know what he was doing. But, of course, one night he began to lose. Badly. Everything he had, and he had markers down for $15,000. That pilot was there, Wade, and he'd brought some fellows from Colombia.

"Ti-Paul took Taffy into the back room, to try to work something out. Ti-Paul and some of the other Haitians run a little loan operation out of the Riverside, but they couldn't do the whole amount. Ti-Paul could raise almost $11,000, but he was wary about making the loan. That's when they called me."

"You?"

"Tommas was there, drinking at the bar. I agreed to put up the other $4,000. It sounded serious for Taffy, what could I say? They wanted cash. I had the money in the house. Tommas and Ti-Paul came over immediately.

"Looking back now, I don't think Taffy ever intended to repay Ti-Paul. He managed to pay me some of what he owed within a few weeks. But the debt to Ti-Paul kept dragging on. Tommas came to see me. Said he had heard if Taffy didn't pay there was going to be a ceremony in the forest; Ti-Paul would throw a curse. Turn Taffy into a slave."

I had to smile.

"That's the drill, you know. They kill the fellow with magic, then bring him back as the undead to be a slave. Like Toussignant."

The rain had stopped. I made a move to leave, but Burnett continued.

"The threat of sorcery was the way Ti-Paul's operation worked. They only loaned to believers. Taffy started receiving messages: a skull and cross chalked on the sidewalk in front of his house, a couple of bloodied white feathers with a rock through the window, ugly printed notes. People began to ignore him; the debt was no longer an issue. The villagers walked past him in the street as if he wasn't there: Madame Dell who does the laundry, Pierre down at the wharf, the fellows at the marina.

"One morning Taffy opened the door of the cottage he'd rented to find a dead chicken nailed to the frame. Its throat had been slit. Blood streaked down the door. There was a cross and a circle of white powder on the steps.

"The next day or two Taffy visited all the merchants. Settling up his bills, the little ones at least. He paid Drover at the grocery store. He paid Mrs. Rainey. He paid Madame Dell, who had complained to everyone that he was weeks behind. He made a great show of it; the whole village saw. I was in town for lunch and met Taffy at the Majestic. I asked him what he was up to.

" 'Voodoo, old boy', he said in a flat voice. 'Afraid I've become a believer.' He looked a little wan. Then he winked. But he never offered to pay me.

"One night, a week later, I heard a drumbeat from the woods. My housekeeper had just brought in the coffee tray and she looked up with a frown. I strolled over to Tommas' place. The drumming was closer than usual, coming from the trees out beyond my tennis court, above the beach path.

"We followed the drumbeat into the woods, further back than it sounded, until we saw light wavering through the trees. The light became brighter. There were storm lanterns hanging from branches around a little clearing with a fire in middle. A figure was dancing, beating the drum and shaking a bone rattle. People approached through the flickering darkness.

"When we had crept to within 25 feet of the fire, Tommas held out his arm. A woman advanced from the shadows into the circle of light, dancing to the beat of the drum. She moved rigidly, wooden. Her face was frozen, her eyes wide. She howled. Another woman came into the circle, then a third. By this time Ti-Paul had put the drum down. He kept up the guttural humming.

"Near the fire was an old oil barrel cut in half, the kind they use to make steel drums, and a pile of broad green leaves and tiny bones. Ti-Paul put the leaves and bones into the oil drum, beating them with a stick. One of the women picked up another stick and began beating along with him. When the contents of the drum had been pounded into powder, the *hougan* knelt and picked up something from the ground. He held it high above his head. A doll-shaped bundle of sticks, around which was knotted Taffy's Racquets Club necktie: a *paquet*. Ti-Paul hurled the *paquet* into the oil drum. The women beat it with their sticks. Ti-Paul threw the whole works into the fire with a wild shout and there was a burst of flame.

"Taffy was in the clinic two days later. He'd been off the island and was in the air over the Berry Islands when the first symptoms appeared. He began to feel faint and nauseated. His skin was cold and moist, his pulse rapid.

"By the time he went into the clinic that evening he was coughing. His blood pressure was low, his red blood count high, he'd lost weight. He asked for me. Naturally I went to see him. By that time he was having difficulty breathing. Said something about a box. Delirious. Then he passed out.

"By morning Taffy was dead, buried the next day. It was late summer so they don't keep bodies long. There was a little service at the Methodist Chapel where Taffy had acted. I heard that there was another ceremony in the woods that night, a ritual meant to guide Taffy safely to the land of the dead."

Burnett paused to relight his pipe.

"You're telling me they killed him with voodoo?" I said.

"You have nothing to worry about. You're not a believer."

"Is the body still in the graveyard?"

"They say not, of course," said Burnett. "They say he lives in the bush somewhere."

Burnett walked to the walkie-talkie that connected him with the out buildings and Tommas' place. A few minutes later I said goodnight and climbed into the jeep, Tommas at the wheel.

"You know anything about a fellow called Mr. Taff?" I said.

"What you want to know?" said Tommas.

"Is his body still in the graveyard?"

He didn't answer immediately. Then he said, "You want to see Mr. Taff?"

Tommas slowed the car to a stop, then threw it into reverse. We turned around and headed south, past the gates to Burnett's long driveway, past the narrows where the Atlantic almost touched the sea, past the fork that led to the cove and Annie's place. We turned several times and soon were driving over rough and rocky tracks between the trees. We drove away from the ocean, away from the cover of the sea grapes and the rustle of the palms. The weather had changed quickly. The ironwood trees and quicksilver bushes looked deathly pale in the light of the half-moon. The trees were taller here; the road narrowed and the moon was soon lost behind a skein of scraggly branches. We lurched to a stop.

"Now we walk," said Tommas.

The going was hard. The islands are ancient coral and I could feel the thin rubber of my moccasins being sliced at every step by the jagged rock. I stopped to catch my breath. The luminous dial on my watch showed a quarter to two.

"Not much further," said Tommas. He pointed.

There were lean-tos of gumwood and spindly pine, a couple of fires and several lanterns around the edge of the camp.

Tommas said a few words in French to a Haitian at the first house. We were led through the ragged village to a hut at the opposite end of the clearing.

Taffy sat on a wooden bench outside the hut. He was round-faced, pink, short and balding; his steel-rimmed glasses glinted in the light of the crackling fire. He wore what would have once been a fine linen suit, now tattered, grey and stained. His mouth was open and there was a raised streak of fleshy skin along his right temple, a badly healed scar. I'd heard about this kind of wound: the mark of a coffin nail.

"Mr. Taff?" I said.

Nothing.

"Taffy? I'm a friend of Burnett's." He stared straight ahead. There was an empty look about him, like an autistic child. Someone spoke in Creole.

"He sleeps most of the day," Tommas said.

"I am a friend of Burnett's," I said again. "I work at the bank."

No change in the blank look. I turned to Tommas.

"He was called back from the dead the night after he was buried. Ti-Paul brought him here."

There was a stirring behind us — Taffy looked up. His lips moved. "The box...." His voice was a raspy whisper. He rose and lunged toward me. There was sweat on his chin, a feral look about the eyes. They restrained him and the frenzy vanished, he stared once more at the ground.

Driving home, Tommas said, "He knew about the magic, how they do it. He was trying to fool the spirits."

I travelled to Nassau every other week to give my paltry reports on Caribbean country analysis: who had oil; who had sugar; how the refineries were doing; trends in the tourism industry. We never mentioned drugs. Coming home from those trips I often stopped at the office across the channel to chat with Healey. I told him Burnett's story.

"Right," said Healey. "Taff knew the whole rigmarole. They do it all with plants and the blood of sea creatures, mashed up bones, stuff like that."

"Plants?"

"Right. Like an anaesthetic. It puts you out for a few days, makes you look dead. They put you in the ground, then they dig you up. Course, you don't want to wake up down there or you'd go mental. A lot of them never recover, especially if they really think they're back from the dead. Walk around slack-jawed, know what I mean?

"How did you know Taff?"

"Came in here trying to get money. Said he was onto a pharmaceutical breakthrough. Then it was some school, money for a nature camp or something. He had a safety deposit box downstairs."

"Is it still there?" I asked.

"You know, another fellow was in here a few months ago asking about Taff's money. Didn't tell him a thing, of course. Bahamian bank law."

Healey opened the box: $55,000 and notes on various types of plants, meticulous notes. He must have made them in London before he came out. There was a description of symptoms: respiratory difficulties, weight loss, hypothermia and hypertension. The poison was topical; you mixed it in a white powder and laid it across the victim's doorway. The drug was absorbed into the bloodstream through the skin.

Several days later, Burnett and I were eating conch fritters and drinking Beck's.

"They were in cahoots," I said. "It was a way for Ti-Paul to get the money he was owed. Taffy planned it from the beginning, even losing that night. They held the ceremony close to the village, where people would hear it and investigate. After that I think it became a question of who was cheating whom."

"A scam — they were in it together?" Burnett said.

"They must have been. Taff had to be certain he would be dug up. Only Ti-Paul could know it was a fake. Taff would die, killed for gambling debts, be buried. The people from whom he'd wheedled money would be out of luck. When he was brought back from the dead, he'd make his way to Marsh Harbour, get the money, pay Ti-Paul and vanish. But something went wrong. He was given too much of the drug, suffered from lack of oxygen down there, I don't know exactly."

Burnett said, "You have an explanation for everything — all this business of topical poisons and comas. I tell you, there are two worlds: the scientific and the spiritual or religious, call it what you like. At some point, those worlds cross over. It's like the Catholic Mass. When does the wine become the Blood of Christ? It all depends upon what you believe. You're right, I said Taffy winked, but that was bravado. I think he half believed even then. Faith is everything. Like fear."

Pigeon Cay, July

I mean to write a story of murder and betrayal. It will be the last of the series. I have been thinking of my past and about the arrangements that people come to, the understandings, both spoken and unspoken. I've also been thinking about the future.

Yesterday I saw Annie sitting on one of the wooden benches in the small park next to the fire station. We had not seen each other for over a week. She was smoking a cigarette. It was uncharacteristic of her, both to be sitting idle in the village like that and to be smoking. It was as though she were waiting for someone. When I approached, she stamped the cigarette out and nodded in the direction of my cottage. She and I walked hand in hand down the Queen's Highway. We sat on my terrace overlooking the entrance to the harbour, sipping drinks. When I got up to make another round, she asked me if I still loved the islands.

I said yes, but in a different way than I had before. I was disillusioned, but protective. I had sense of proprietorship.

She followed me into the house. Two hours later we woke up in one another's arms. How did this happen: I'm in love with her, sometimes even think I could marry her and take her back to Canada. But I don't want just to be part of a plan, a means for Annie and Azalea to get away. I am not a fool. Are people never happy with what they have?

Eleven

The first victim was one of the itinerants who lived in the bush at the southern end of the island. People in the village knew him because they sometimes saw him at the ferry dock, helping tourists with their luggage. He'd been noticed visiting Madame Dell, who lived with her stepdaughter in a neat little house behind the Majestic Hotel. He walked with a swagger and wore a red bandanna. He was about 20. Apart from that, no one knew much about him.

"Probably a squabble over rum," said Burnett.

The police showed little interest in the matter because the Haitians were not as a rule involved in the drug trade. They had no shiny new boats or fancy clothes like those of the young men who frequented the Riverside Tavern. Besides, the victim had been knifed — the long draw of a serrated edge across the throat — and guns, not knives, were the weapons of choice in the drug trade.

The body was found near a trail running through the gumwood trees to Fish Mangrove, where many of the illegals first came ashore. It made a good spot for the little boats to land unseen and unheard. He was found by a tourist, someone from the hotel exploring the island.

The dead man had lived in a hut not far from Burnett's

property, out where the bush was slowly taking over the last of the citrus plantations.

Constable MacMahon had been out to see him the day after the murder was discovered and then Burnett came to see me at the bank, expressly to relate the story.

"I knew Pierre, of course," Burnett said, "but he didn't work for me. Not regularly, anyway. Helped out with big jobs once in a while, repaired my river pier last spring. A lot of them live out there, you know. Some actually on my property, some not. I told Constable MacMahon he was welcome to go out and have a look around. When he came back to the house afterward — walked right through my bloody papayas — he said he'd be coming to see you. Don't know why."

MacMahon ambled into the bank that afternoon just before closing time. He was a very large man. Even though he'd lived in the islands all his life, he seemed never to have gotten used to the heat. He was our only police officer. He was sweating heavily.

"Recognize this?"

He threw onto my desk a bank passbook. I saw the plastic cover with the address of the local branch embossed on the front, put there with the stamping machine we'd acquired in Nassau at great expense.

Constable MacMahon said the passbook belonged to Pierre. "I found it on a shelf above his bed," he said. He looked at me and waited.

"You need a court order for me to open bank records," I said.

"You tell me if I should bother getting one," said Constable MacMahon.

He removed his hat and wiped the top of his large pale head

with a handkerchief. While I was looking through the files, he continued.

"Pierre had nothing worth stealing. He never carried much money. No watch, no jewellery. Madame Dell's stepdaughter told me that."

I looked up at this, as though to ask a question.

"There was an understanding between them," he said. "The stepdaughter was at the hotel until almost midnight and she was home with Madame Dell after that," said Constable MacMahon. "So it wasn't her."

Madame Dell's stepdaughter was a waitress at the Majestic Hotel. She had a reputation for keeping to herself, almost sullen; I was surprised she had come to an understanding; in the Haitian community that usually meant marriage.

"There's nothing unusual in his bank transactions," I said. To save Constable MacMahon the trouble of reading the figures upside down, I flipped the page half around on my desk, then waited while he fumbled in the breast pocket of his shirt for his bifocals.

"Lump sum deposits every now and then." I pointed out the figures with a pencil. "Not so very large, really. That would be consistent with payment for the jobs he did. I believe he rebuilt Burnett's dock last summer."

Of the few Haitian families that had houses in the village, Madame Dell's was the most prosperous. Her husband had been a professional man, educated in France, who had run afoul of the Duvaliers. She was trained as a nurse. As well as taking in laundry, she worked several days a week looking after an old woman from Connecticut who had a villa out on North Point.

I hadn't known Pierre and I was inclined to agree with Burnett that it was probably some trivial dispute, the settlement of which had been inflamed by liquor.

I mentioned the murder to Madame Dell one morning when she was delivering my laundered sheets. A shadow crossed her face.

"Mr. Rennison, I don't know nothing about it," she said, "but that man, he was no good." She paused. "Always chasing the women."

Winnie Macdonald hinted at the same thing, as did the villagers at Drover's grocery store.

And then Healey came over on the ferry from regional head office in Nassau for his weekly visit. I met him walking up the steps from the government dock with two bottles of rum. The men who worked on the ferry had told him about Pierre's death and he added his own theory about motive.

"He was a prostitute. That's what they say. Local girl got in the way of some tourist's crush."

The second murder was two and a half weeks later. Mrs. Rainey, delivering conch to Madame Dell, as she did every Thursday night after the fishing boats came in, heard the stepdaughter wail as she came into the kitchen from the hotel. Madame Dell had been stabbed through the heart.

There was fear on the island. Pierre had been a drifter. This was different. Her house was not 50 yards from where I sat in the bank.

That night the tourists remained snug aboard their yachts and locked behind the wooden shutters of their cabins and hotel rooms. The villagers stayed home and the paths that wound through the village were empty. At the Terrace Bar there was no clinking of ice in rum punches on the patio, no banging of Beck's bottles on the table tops, no chatter of voices, only the clicking of the palm fronds in the Atlantic winds.

I saw Constable MacMahon in the post office.

"What was it this time?"

"Ritual killing," he said darkly.

At the Yacht Club there was a talk of exerting influence on the capital to garner more attention, to get to the bottom of it. A day or two later men came from across the channel to take photographs, fingerprints and measurements.

Constable MacMahon came to my house on Sunday morning. I was in bed when he knocked and I answered the door in my robe.

"Sorry to wake you, Mr. Rennison. I wonder if we could talk."

"Now?"

"It's about Madame Dell."

He was looking for financial records.

"All these fellows coming from across the channel. Cameras and powders. Can't touch anything. You'll have to come with me."

When we arrived at Madame Dell's, people were gathered around, watching. The Roman Catholic service was over — it was held under the tree at the foot of the government dock — and the entire congregation seemed to have come by afterward.

" 'Scuse me, 'scuse me," he said gruffly, elbowing his way through the crowd. I followed close behind.

Madame Dell's house was small and tidy. I'd never been inside before. We entered by the door that faced the harbour and went up a narrow staircase where two little bedrooms and a bathroom jammed under the sloping roof. I watched while Constable MacMahon went through the contents of the bureau in Madame Dell's room. There were some letters, mostly written in French, one or two old legal documents, also in French, and the bank passbook. There was a chequebook, but I told Constable MacMahon not to bother with it, for business on the out islands is conducted almost entirely in cash and the cheques had hardly been used.

Back downstairs, the kitchen was crowded with the police who had come in by boat earlier in the morning. The body had been removed (taken over to Marsh Harbour, where they had a morgue), but there were dark brown-red stains on the unpainted wooden table and on the floor where the men were working.

"You know anyone around here who could translate for us?" he asked.

"Most of the Haitians speak English," I said.

"It's translation of *written* material we need," said the policeman.

"Fellow called Tommas who lives out by Burnett's place," I said. "He's an educated man."

Constable MacMahon and I left by the kitchen door. Behind the house there was a steep bank, covered with scruffy vegetation, leading to the back garden of the Majestic. A cement walk led from the kitchen door around to the front of the house.

"What about the stepdaughter?" I asked. "Where was she this time?"

"Working at the hotel. I saw her myself. Dropped in at the dart tournament after dinner. They said she didn't leave until almost midnight, when Mrs. Rainey met her."

"She could have slipped out the back, climbed down the bank here and been back before anyone noticed," I said.

"I suppose it's possible," said Constable MacMahon, casting an eye up the hill.

At Constable MacMahon's insistence we went directly to the bank. As with Pierre's account, I found nothing particularly unusual. The balance was larger than might have been expected, but I'd heard before that Madame Dell was one of the Haitians who had brought money with her. There were regular small deposits, more or less regular small withdrawals, and four or five larger withdrawals.

"Probably for laundry supplies," I said to Constable MacMahon, "and larger purchases of some kind."

The balance had declined somewhat over the past few months. Constable MacMahon stared blankly at the upside-down figures for a few moments, grunted and left the bank without saying a word.

For all their photographs, fingerprint taking, officious scrutiny, tape measuring and what we later learned was blood type analysis, the police from New Providence did no better than Constable MacMahon at solving the murders.

I was on the ferry on my way to the airport for one of my trips to Miami when I met Tommas. He was travelling to New Providence for a meeting of a left-wing exile group.

I made some reference to Madame Dell's stepdaughter. She was no longer required to remain for questioning and was planning to leave the islands. No doubt the decision was inspired by the money she had been left.

"Man, it has nothing to do with the money," Tommas said. "She has been dishonoured."

On the plane to Miami I thought about Tommas' remark. I thought about the look on Madame Dell's face when I'd asked her about Pierre. I thought about Winnie, telling me the village gossip.

I flew back to Marsh Harbour in the afternoon and took a

water taxi across the channel to the village. In the evening I walked along the path past Burnett's place, through the silvery woods to Tommas's hut. The barking of a German shepherd brought him outside. He calmed the dog. He invited me in.

"It's about the translations you did for the police who came over from Nassau," I said. He shrugged his shoulders, then led me to the wooden table in the corner of the room.

The details were there, in those letters that had been on Madame Dell's bureau. I laboriously went over Tommas' translations. The money had been provided to Madame Dell by the family of her husband — the girl's father — and was to be paid to Pierre in six installments, the final payment on the day of the marriage.

"Did she love him?" I said.

"I would say so," said Tommas. "She slept with him."

"A dowry?" said Burnett. We were at the Terrace Bar. The waiter brought our drinks, gin and soda for him, beer for me.

"Which Pierre had almost certainly already spent," I said.

"And the girl killed her mother?"

"Not her mother. Her stepmother. Her wicked stepmother, the person who had killed her lover. Perhaps she found the knife. Who knows?"

"Imagine Madame Dell murdering the fellow for that amount of money in the first place."

"I don't think it was the money," I said. "It was bad enough that he was seeing other women. He had dishonoured her, dishonoured the family. He broke his promise, a breach of contract, but with no recourse to a court of law. So Madame Dell followed him into the mangroves where he used to meet her stepdaughter and killed him in the darkness."

"How do you know all this?"

"I don't know for certain. But it's in the figures."

I had returned to the bank immediately after visiting Tommas. I took Madame Dell's and Pierre's accounts from the files and quickly compared them. The large withdrawals from Madame Dell's account were followed in all cases a day or two later by deposits in his. Four of Pierre's deposits were identical to her withdrawals and the fifth was only slightly less.

"Why don't you go the police?" Burnett asked.

"For the same reason I don't go to the U.S. tax department about you."

"How's that?" Burnett bridled a little, so I quoted the law.

" 'No person under Bahamian jurisdiction is permitted to divulge bank information obtained in the course of his or her employment.' It protects us all," I said.

A few days later Madame Dell's stepdaughter came to see me at my office. She withdrew all her own money — she would have to wait for the lawyers to get the inheritance — and then she left the bank and the island, too, for Miami.

It was a matter of professional curiosity. Before closing the file, I went over the record of transactions in her account. I realized then that what I had told Burnett was wrong, that Tommas, too, had been mistaken. There in the figures were five large deposits. I knew without checking that the amounts were the same as the amounts withdrawn from Madame Dell's account. Madame Dell must have discovered what they were up to — an elaborate collaboration to get what I suppose the stepdaughter saw as rightfully hers. It was not a question of honour and love. I should have guessed, for I was no poet; it was the money after all.

Pigeon Cay, August

I have been on this island over two years. What has changed?

The wildlife is in retreat. There are less conch, fewer lobsters, less forest, fewer stretches of mangrove shoreline. Out in the reef, a relentless diminution, from souvenir hunters and pollution. The sewage in the harbour stinks more than ever. We're ruining the place. Even the packs of stray dogs seem smaller than when I arrived. In summer, when the tourists are gone, people in the interior eat them.

And like everywhere else on the planet, there are more people. People on their way to the U.S.: Haitians, Cubans, Salvadoreans, Nicaraguans, almost all of them here illegally. And tourists in a mass visitation, like locusts. (I exclude myself, of course). Rich retirees. More building on the coastlines, more and more garish houses. Next year, cruise ships. In the interior, more huts, shacks of cardboard and plastic sheeting. The poor leave a smaller footprint; their lives are taken up with getting food and sullen rage.

And at the bank, just as suddenly as it came, the business is gone. Cash deposits are way off; they may even close us down.

Gregor Robinson

The official reason is the competition from across the channel. The real reason is that the smugglers are using other means of shipment, other points of entry. Scared off by all those planes glittering overhead, drug enforcement agents, or police, or the Defence Force. Some were from Immigration Services, so Ed Holder tells me. Turns out that's the big story he's working on.

Some paradise.

On Sunday Drover told us that Jerusalem was built on a high plain. As you approach, whether by air or by land, the city is visible for miles. The outskirts are ringed by the concrete structures; they have a Soviet look, as though designed by the master builders of a people's democratic republic. But closer to the old city, you begin to see the domes and spires. You see the churches, the synagogues, the mosques, the Dome of the Rock, sacred places. So many pilgrimages.

I helped Annie get her papers in order. I am to meet her in Miami. We don't know exactly when she'll arrive, so I'll wait for her there. I didn't marry her. Not yet. I explained that that would be unfair to her and Azalea, to me, to whatever future we might have. Instead, I enlisted Burnett and the powers that be at the bank to help her get out. She won't be anyone's human cargo, won't have to go across by raft or small boat.

How long will I wait?

Twelve

I lay in a tropical illness. Nausea, cramps, fever: the reaction to the touch of one of the strange plants which grew in the forests behind the village; or to the hallucinogenic blossoms that flourished, untended, in the lurid garden beneath my window where the banana quits fluttered; or to the dreamy caress of the emerald arms that beckoned from the filtered sunlight of the ocean floor, or to the venom of the sea anemone or another of the tiny spined creatures that lived in the reef; or perhaps to the sun.

Upon my arrival at Pigeon Cay, almost three years ago, I had taken to the beach and burned my face so badly that my skin exuded a clear, orange liquid for several days. I was treated with ointments and shade, and have since been unable to spend more than brief periods in the sun.

I lay in the living room, the coolest place in the house, and gazed at the green light through the slats of the shutters, waiting for the weather to break.

I should have called the doctor, but it was only a fight. That's how it began, a fistfight in a bar — no need to bring the doctor in for that sort of thing. Refined Dr. Cutter, trained at McGill, what would she have done but view with disgust a cut lip and those flowers of blood around the eyes?

For the first time in over two years, I was lonely. Annie had taken Azalea and gone to join her mother on one of the main islands; they were waiting for the paperwork to clear.

The illness had started with a fight, but like an opportunistic virus or an introduced species it had transformed itself into something else: a kind of melancholy, a new way of seeing. Once, in a dessert campsite in New Mexico, a scorpion bit me. It was like that, the puffiness and fever. I was unhinged.

Or was it merely torpor, the unnaturally hot days? It was late August. The weather was freakish, the ocean breezes gone; the only movement of air on the entire island came from the ceiling fans of bars and a few ancient air conditioners.

At Cape Hatteras, 800 miles to the north, a storm was gathering, moving eastward, and the seas were starting to build.

It was the weather, but it was also the season; the tourists were gone, the hotels were empty. Most of the part-time expatriates had gone back to Vermont, Connecticut, New York, to their country houses in England, in Canada. Later, in the dog days of summer, illegal Haitian workers might come out of the bush or across the channel to repair and renovate, but for now the great oceanside villas, the pink-and-pastel green cottages, were shuttered tight.

The lagoon was almost empty. Later, we might have sailors, real sailors, who navigated their own boats down the coast and across the Gulf Stream, not the millionaires who chartered fantastic yachts in the winter, but for now the lagoon was almost empty. Two of the marinas had closed for the season. Business was flat.

The drug trade had abandoned us as well, vanished for good; entrepreneurial smugglers had started flying their light planes straight to Florida, then into Louisiana, Alabama, Texas or sailing their ships up to the Carolinas, to Maine, as far north as Nova Scotia.

Ed Holder was from Toronto, older than I was, maybe 45. He'd originally been a friend of Karen's. We used to talk about books. He was a precise person. There was never a crease or a smudge on his jacket. War correspondents were supposed to suck back the Marlboros, but Ed Holder didn't smoke. He had this way of pursing his lips.

There was something else we had in common, besides Karen and a dilettantish interest in literature. ("That guy's read more books than anyone I've ever met," said Healey. "Is he gay, or what?") We had both fled. We were both refugees, in pursuit of the exotic. The rumour was Ed lived with a girl in Old Havana. We had never been close and I had not been glad to see him.

I had been taken aback when he had come into the bank, unannounced. He had been in a camouflage flak jacket, all pockets and buttons, and heavy-duty shoes.

"You're a walking cliché," I told him. "You've seen too many movies. Read too many books. You look like a war correspondent."

"I *am* a war correspondent."

"Oh? Where is the war in the Bahamas? Let me guess — the drug war. You're hot on the trail of the Medellin Cartel."

"I've come from Haiti."

"You stayed at the Hotel Oloffson, a gingerbread mansion of towers and cupolas. You took dinner on the old verandas, festooned...." It was a game we played, these references to novels, literary allusions.

"Festooned?" said Ed as we strolled over to the lobby of the Majestic.

"Festooned, absolutely, Don't interrupt. Festooned with bougainvillaea, overlooking the unkempt garden, dangerous and foreboding at night. The swimming pool was empty. Perhaps there was a corpse. You drank by yourself in the bar. In the morning, you strolled up to the lush heights above the town, to Petionville, where the corrupt and wealthy live, behind their garden walls, dogs straining on chains. Back at the waterfront, you searched out voodoo — *voudon*, you call it — and were disappointed to learn that visitors are welcome to the ceremonies, that the hotels arrange regular excursions. You strolled through the market, taking in the smells. In the late afternoon, you returned to the Oloffson. You felt cleansed by the tropical rain. You rested before dinner between crisp white sheets. You awoke, refreshed, excited. After dinner and your customary session in the bar, you sat on the veranda in the moonlight, too restless to sleep. You could hardly wait to get into the hills the next day to see the poor, the destruction they've done to their land, and the evil that's been done to them. You wished, somehow, you could be more — committed."

"You've been there?" said Ed.

"Never. But I'm an exile myself. *The Comedians*, by the way. Graham Greene."

"When did you become such a cynic?"

In doing "Latin American Country Analysis" for the bank, I'd learned that thousands of Latin Americans entered North America every day. The flight northward was ceaseless. And it was going on all over the world: in eastern and southern Europe, Mexico and India, in Ethiopia and Somalia, throughout Africa. Where did the few hundred Haitians and the fewer Cubans who came here fit in all that? Even people who were not starving and not being persecuted were on the move. Look at me. Look at Ed.

"How long have they been coming here?"

"Years. Centuries. Columbus first. Looking for the green light at the end of Daisy's dock, the green breast of the new world. They came long before the unfulfilled, dreamy foreign correspondents arrived with their tropical luggage at the Hotel Oloffson in Port-au-Prince."

I poured myself another drink from the bottle of *ron añejo* the barman had placed before us.

"There's another myth, isn't there, Dave?" Dave! How I hated being called Dave. "Even more juvenile than the foreign correspondent. The dissipated expatriate. Humphrey Bogart, maybe? Malcolm Lowry."

"Not Malcolm Lowry — too pathological. Go with Paul Theroux, or Somerset Maugham. He was the original."

"Anyway, it's not the Oloffson I'm interested in," Ed said. "It's the Hotel Paradiso."

"Home of monster cockroaches and German tourists. They let them go nude on the beach there. What do you want at the Hotel Paradiso?"

He shrugged, playing things close to the vest. "A story I'm working on."

"A story? Ed, there is no story at the Hotel Paradiso. It's the Riverside Tavern you want. That's where the drug buyers go. Or the Goombay Bar. Gambling. Cocaine traders doing business with your Colombians drink there. Cigarette boats carry the stuff to Miami. End of the reef, lee side of the island, can't miss it."

"How did you get into a fight, anyway?" asked Ed. "You're not the kind of guy who would be in a place like that at one o'clock in the morning."

"Jay McInerney," I said. "Hardly up to your standards, I would've thought. And shouldn't the author be dead? Isn't that the rule?"

"So sorry," said Ed.

"I used to box, when I was at university, at Hart House. I've sparred occasionally with Healey here, on the beach, once even at a gym, over at Marsh Harbour. Tommas somehow knew that."

"Writers who box," said Ed. "Like Hemingway and Fitzgerald."

"Hemingway and Morley Callaghan, you mean; Fitzgerald was the timekeeper. And Tommas doesn't box; he fights. You should have been there. You could have been timekeeper. Where were you?"

"I was in the bush, talking to the Haitians in the refugee settlements."

"Did you find out anything?" I asked.

"No."

"What did I tell you?"

"I know something's going on. They're afraid. That's why they won't talk."

"You talk to Burnett, the fellows at the Yacht Club?" I said.

"They're a bunch of racists, waiting for something to happen," said Ed. "A riot, something."

"*Burmese Days*," I said. "George Orwell."

"So, what were you doing in that bar?"

"Drinking. What else?"

It was as though we were waiting for something to happen, so we drank, but it was too hot too hot to drink outside at the Terrace Bar, so we drank inside, in the windowless lobby of the Majestic Hotel (they had a species of air conditioner there), or at the Riverside Tavern, built on wooden pilings above the harbour. Through a hole in the floor you could see the pulsating jellyfish that thrived on the sewage.

Ed said, "Weather like this — it can't last. Something's got to happen."

"Maybe it's an asteroid," I said. "Heating Earth as it hurtles into the atmosphere, like an exploding sun. We have a day to go before it all ends, day and a half at most."

I lay back on the wicker chesterfield, my arm across my forehead. I could almost see that bursting sun.

"Where's that from?" said Ed. "Not J.G. Ballard. Something by John Wyndham?"

"Rod Sterling. *The Twilight Zone*. This guy can't get warm, he's freezing to death. Then he wakes up, looks out the window, sees the sun, getting closer and closer."

I reached over to the basin of cool water on the floor. "If you'd been there with me, you might have learned something — about the Hotel Paradiso."

"That is what your fight was about?" said Ed.

"Yes, in a way. I think it was."

I had been in the fetid lobby of the Majestic Hotel on the third night of the heat wave. Bottles glowed in the yellow light behind the bar. Red and yellow streamers rippled out from the air conditioner above the doorway. Seymour Dufresne, Ti-Paul and Tommas were drinking Wray and Nephew, clear overproof from Jamaica — the cheapest rum in the bar.

Ti-Paul said, "Hey bass, business bad?"

I shrugged.

"Least you got a job."

I was starting to hate my desk in the bank overlooking the harbour as much as I had hated my desk in Montreal and those long grey corridors. But it was true, I had a job and it would have been churlish to say more.

I sat at the bar, drinking. Tommas was looking at me. When he turned to me, I assumed it would be to talk about writing.

He said, "You still lending money to those Nazis at the Hotel Paradiso?"

"Norwegians, not Nazis. And it's only a revolving line of credit. Working capital. They repay like clockwork."

Tommas said, "You like to box, *bass*?" an unnatural emphasis on a word he never used. "Bass, you box, I said?"

"Oh, it's nothing. Used to do a little. I'm out of practice."

"Do me the honour. Spar with me."

I'd be happy to, I told him. I meant some time, in the future. But Tommas had risen from his chair. He folded his glasses and put them on the table.

"Here? Now?"

"It would be a great honour." By then I knew that it was not honour he was interested in. I had 20 pounds on him, but I was afraid.

I said, "The room is air-conditioned. Why not?"

In boxing I had one move, or sequence of moves: I would guard with my left, jabbing, waiting for the chance to throw an uppercut with my right. It had worked at Hart House and it worked with Healey. But I was flat with Tommas. His big punch was his left. My guard was useless, and I didn't know how to adapt. He danced around for a few seconds, snapping at my midriff, then he connected with my right eye. I wobbled, felt warm blood. The room tilted. I jabbed but didn't touch him. There were two more hits, one to my mouth, one to the other eye. Tommas was using both hands. He held his arms low, a sign of contempt. With the final blow, I fell to the floor. It was over in perhaps a minute. I had not hurt him once.

Tommas put on his glasses and left. Vero came around from behind the bar with a towel, helped me to my feet. Seymour and Ti-Paul looked down at me from their table, expressionless, no longer jovial. I was wheezing. The smell of beer and old cigarettes on the floor of that bar...I thought I would vomit.

"I'm a little out of practice," I said.

"No shit, Great White Father," said Seymour.

"So it was about the Hotel Paradiso, how you lend to them but not to Seymour Dufresne," said Ed.

"A matter of policy," I said. "At the bank, we have a thing called 'loan criteria.'"

"How does the hotel keep going?" asked Ed.

People were waiting for someone to develop the Hotel Paradiso, turn it into a Club Med, but there were no buyers.

"Is it possible," said Ed, "that you don't apply your 'loan criteria' to European hotel owners in the same way you do to Haitian refugees?"

"It is possible," I said.

"They have a pier there, at the Hotel Paradiso?"

"They have."

"Freighters dock there?"

"Occasionally. Only place on the island they can tie up, drop off building supplies, minivans and the like. Occasionally the *Violet Mitchell* on its weekly run from West Palm. Others from time to time."

"I think I know how they make their money," said Ed.

"I thought you'd say that. You reporters. Clever."

"Yes, and I've been here what — not quite a week? You've been here over two years."

Gregor Robinson

The hotel itself was set in a perfect half-moon bay, a crescent of white sand fringed by a row of royal palms. Here the sea was still and clear. Angelfish and giant rays swam along the bottom. The pier extended almost to the middle of the bay, so that yachts sailing the passage might stop.

But few did. The shore was jagged with the hulks of derelict cars and trucks and empty oil drums. There was an old bulldozer and a heap of ossified asphalt (someone had once planned to build a go-cart track). The hotel was concrete, streaky grey with a dull blue metal roof. Scattered in the unkempt growth behind were cement block cottages with incongruous thatch roofs, and behind those, a thin stream of smoke from a bonfire.

We approached as the sun sank behind the silhouette of forest. Ed had shamed me into accompanying him. Besides, my health was improving, the nights were cooler and I could not lie on my chesterfield forever. As we tied the outboard to the pier, we noticed something dark and looming in the dusk of the middle channel. A freight boat, the MV *April Gallagher*.

Swan, the hotel owner, and the captain of the *April Gallagher* were both Norwegian. The captain was originally a whaler, who had moved to the United States years before. (This was reported later in the Miami papers.)

They were sitting at a table by an open window in the lounge and looked up as we walked by. The captain turned to Swan, as though to ask a question.

"It's only my banker," said Swan. "Not come to collect, have you? Join us?"

I declined. There was no air-conditioning here. The walls were streaked with moisture.

"Who is your friend?" asked Swan.

"This is Mr. Holder," I said. "A client from Montreal. He's interested in resort properties. May we look around?"

Swan considered a moment. He said, "Is Mr. Holder as discreet as you are?"

"Absolutely."

"Then go ahead. We have only four guests at the moment. Try not to disturb them."

I showed Ed the lounge, the kitchens, the cottages, two of which appeared to be occupied. Then I waited for him on the small rise behind the hotel. People came here to watch the launch of the space shuttles from Cape Canaveral, 80 miles to the west. There would be a pale green flash in the morning sky as the booster rocket burst away.

From the back of the hotel, Ed beckoned me, then called. It was becoming hard to see in the fading light. Nearby, a Haitian worker threw rubbish onto the bonfire.

"Something to show you," Ed said. I followed him around the side to a basement stairwell. He opened one of the wooden doors. Cool, mildewy air wafted up as we descended.

There were perhaps 30 people in the basement. They sat huddled on the dirt floor. I didn't recognize any of them. These were people who had never ventured from the settlements into the village. How long had they been here? How long had they been waiting for passage? None could speak English. A few had suitcases, many had green garbage bags. A young woman held a child in her arms. The basement smelled overpoweringly of urine.

"I grant you, this is peculiar," I said to Ed. I began to sweat. My fever threatened. My eyes hurt. "Let's get out of here."

Outside, clouds moved across the face of the moon. At last a breeze was rising.

Ed asked how long refugees had been on the island. I

couldn't tell him. No one had seen the first Haitians disembark and drag themselves through the stinky mud of Fish Mangrove. One day they were simply there. We only knew they worked cheap — a few dollars a day — and did work that few others would do: clearing the bush for a new house, a banana plantation, a stand of papayas; quarrying the razor-sharp coral; washing or peeling at the kitchen sinks of resort hotels.

August 20th dawned beautiful, the air cooler. The weather and my fever broke. But there was something strange: the Atlantic was almost half a mile away across the hump of the peninsula, yet I could hear a steady roar. A rage sea was up.

The first reports came crackling over the citizens' band at one in the afternoon. Ed Holder insisted we take the outboard and have a look.

There are two stretches on the Pigeon Cay-South Florida run where ships are at risk — the Gulf Stream and Whale Cay passage. Sailors are prepared for the Gulf Stream. Whale Cay is different. It is the only part of the passage between the islands and the Gulf Stream where ships must enter the open ocean. The rest of the way is protected by the reef and the islands along Little Bahamas Bank. Whale Cay is one of the few places where the offshore reef is interrupted, and the ocean floor rises, so that the channel and the Atlantic come together in shallow waters, creating the potential for large breaking seas.

There were no buoys, no aids to navigation here. The waves were 25 feet high, flecked with foam. We would have to turn back momentarily. Ed shouted at me from the front of the boat, but I could not hear him over the roar. Then he pointed. He had his story.

The *April Gallagher* was a hundred and 160 with a 25-foot beam and a draft of ten feet, and she wallowed upside down in the main shipping lane at the north end of Whale Cay. The bow remained above the water, brown and splotchy.

Air-Sea Rescue came later and picked up the survivors: the captain and all but one of the crew of six. The rage that day was the result of a buildup of water from heavy seas off George's Bank and Cap May, a thousand miles away. It was a surge that moved toward the islands at a speed of over 600 miles a day, 30 miles an hour. The stern of *April Gallagher* had been lifted out of the water as she came back into the inner passage. Without her rudder, the ship broached and rolled upside down in an instant.

I wondered what they had seen as they sailed north that morning, the air clear, the long green cays shimmering to the east, the small islands to the west low and light compared to the hills of Haiti. They would have seen the turquoise sea, the candy-striped lighthouse, the pastel villas among the wispy pines, the cut-out of the high palms.

They would have been below, straining to see through the portholes. There would have been silence except for the throb of the engines. In the air, the sea-salt freshness, and a whiff of diesel fumes assuring them that they were steaming northward, away from the islands.

Behind the Hotel Paradiso, I walked through the remains of the bonfire: plastic bags and suitcases and ragged clothing which nobody could possibly have wanted. Some old furniture. A television set. They had been allowed to bring one bag each.

I gazed out to sea, toward the green light of West Palm Beach, the Florida Gold Coast, the strip-plaza continent that stretched away from there. I knew what it was that I had been waiting for.

Acknowledgements

Excerpts from this novel have previously been published in slightly different form in *Descant*, *Blood & Aphorisms*, *Ellery Queen*, and *Alfred Hitchcock Mystery Magazine*. I would like to thank Oakland Ross, Sheila Robinson, George Fallis and W. Pitblado for their support.

The image used for the cover illustration is a detail from the painting *Pacific* by Alex Colville (1968): acrylic polymer emulsion, 53.3 x 53.3 cm, private collection. It is used with permission of the artist.